THE CASTLE

ON

CURTIS PARKINSON

DEADMAN'S ISLAND

TUNDRA BOOKS

Published in Canada by Tundra Books,
75 Sherbourne Street, Toronto, Ontario M5A 2P9

Published in the United States by Tundra Books of Northern New York,
P.O. Box 1030, Plattsburgh, New York 12901

Library of Congress Control Number: 2008903010

Library and Archives Canada Cataloguing in Publication

Parkinson, Curtis
    The castle on Deadman's Island / Curtis Parkinson.

ISBN 978-0-88776-893-4

    I. Title.

PS8581.A76234C34 2009   jC813'.54   C2008-902057-X

We acknowledge the financial support of the Government of Canada
through the Book Publishing Industry Development Program (BPIDP)
and that of the Government of Ontario through the Ontario Media
Development Corporation's Ontario Book Initiative. We further
acknowledge the support of the Canada Council for the Arts and the
Ontario Arts Council for our publishing program.

Design: Scott Richardson
Typeset in: Dante

ONTARIO ARTS COUNCIL
CONSEIL DES ARTS DE L'ONTARIO

Printed and bound in Canada

1 2 3 4 5 6   14 13 12 11 10 09

To Anne, Geoff, and Jane

ACKNOWLEDGMENTS

The best stories, as someone wisely said, are not created; they are discovered by the author as they unfold on the page. I'm grateful to those who helped so much along the way as I was discovering, sometimes to my surprise, this story.

Particular thanks to Kathy Lowinger, Sue Tate, and Anne Carter. My thanks, too, to the staff at Tundra, who so skillfully made this book a reality.

THE CASTLE ON
DEADMAN'S ISLAND

PREFACE

The castle towered menacingly over the bottle green pines and the royal blue waters of the St. Lawrence River. It was said to be cursed.

Built by an American millionaire on Deadman's Island in the early years of the twentieth century, its picturesque setting was unequaled. But at the party to celebrate the opening, a prominent guest fell off the dock and drowned. Then, in 1929, the millionaire owner lost his fortune overnight in the stock-market crash and leapt to his death from the tower.

When the young son of the next owner disappeared mysteriously from the castle one day, never to be seen again, the curse of the Castle on Deadman's Island was entrenched forever in local lore.

ONE

Neil Graves was convinced that someone was after his friend. Yet Graham was making light of it. "Did you get the license number?" Neil asked.

"The car was gone before I had a chance," Graham said. "I only saw the color – dark green – and the driver's hat. Anyway, it's my own fault. I was thinking about something else and I wasn't looking."

They crossed the street and headed for the high school. Neil noticed that Graham looked carefully both ways this time. He's more concerned than he's letting on, he thought, and he's not telling me the whole story.

Typical Graham. I'll have to pry the details out of him.

"But the girls said the car swerved right at you," Neil said. "Like it was trying to run you down. . . ."

Graham sneezed. The ragweed season was back and so was his hay fever. "Those girls hab a tendency to drabatize."

The mysterious note in the library book, the man spying on Graham, the careening car . . . to Neil, it all sounded sinister and threatening. "I don't like it."

Graham pulled out a large red handkerchief and blew his nose. "I didn't look where I was going, that's all – I was pondering the future of television."

"Telewhat?"

"Television. It's a new invention – like radio with pictures. They say it'll be in every living room after the war. Forget radio."

Neil was skeptical. Forget radio! Forget *The Shadow; Jack Armstrong, the All-American Boy*; Jack Benny; Bob Hope! "Who says so?"

"I read all about it in *Popular Mechanics*," Graham said. Neil could almost smell the chalk as Graham switched into professor mode. "Quite simple, really. The pictures from the television camera are turned into electrical impulses called pixels, which are beamed through the air to a picture tube in your living room, and –"

"The man driving the car," Neil interrupted, not caring about pixels right now, "he was the same guy who was spying on you in the library?"

"No. What I said was, the driver of the car wore a gray fedora, like the guy in the library. I didn't say he was the same guy."

"Come on, Graham. Someone's secretly watching you in the library, and half an hour later, someone's trying to run you down in the street. And they have the same hat. Funny coincidence."

"Oh, I don't know. There's lots of gray fedoras in Kingsport. Besides, why would anyone want to run me down?"

Right then and there, Neil decided he'd better stick close to Graham for a while. If his best friend wasn't going to watch out for himself, then he, Neil, darn well better. Without letting on to Graham, of course.

TWO

It had started in the Kingsport Library the day before. The library's polished walnut woodwork lent it a warmth that invited you to sit and read a novel, or browse through the latest issue of a magazine – perhaps *Time*, with its eyewitness account of the thousand-plane bombing of Germany the week before; or *Life*'s action photos from the deck of an American aircraft carrier, with guns blazing at Japanese kamikaze planes hurtling towards it.

Graham Graham, however, wasn't interested in a novel or a magazine on this June afternoon in 1942.

He was in the library's reference room, looking for a book on castles.

Miss McKnight, the librarian, had been surprised. Graham's usual requests were for some obscure book on mathematics, or physics, or geology that most teenagers would never have heard of. His vocabulary wasn't what you'd expect to hear from a teenager, either – it was peppered with words like "tome" for book or "dilatory" for late. Not that he was trying to impress anyone – that was just the way he was. At school he was generally shunned, except for his friend Neil.

"There's a book on castles in the reference room," Miss McKnight had said, giving him the Dewey decimal number, "but it can't be taken out. You'll have to read it here.

"That's odd," she said to her assistant, as she watched Graham trot off to the reference room. "That book on castles has been sitting on the shelf for years, untouched, and now Graham is the second person today to ask for it. . . ."

As Graham was taking the thick book down from the top shelf, a creepy feeling overwhelmed him. The back of his neck tingled. He knew someone was watching.

He turned. Through one of the slits between the rows of shelved books behind him, he caught a glimpse of steely eyes peering intently at him. Just a glimpse and they were gone.

He had an uneasy moment, then shrugged and went back to the book. He was interested in it because his aunt Henrietta had just inherited a castle, or rather, one-third of a castle. Until then, the only castle Graham ever had anything to do with was the one in Shakespeare's *Macbeth*. He'd had a small part in the play when the high-school drama group recruited him to be one of the castle flunkies.

"'Double, double, toil and trouble; Fire burn, and cauldron bubble,'" he remembered the witches in the play chanting, foretelling the bloody events to come in that gloomy Scottish castle. Not a good omen for his aunt if *that* was any indication of what went on in castles, he thought.

Now, searching through the book, he found that most of the castles in it were ancient, like Macbeth's, and situated in strategic places for defense against invaders. His aunt's castle, however, was relatively new as castles go and was originally built as a million-aire's summer retreat. It was, in fact, just down the river from Kingsport.

"Her castle probably won't even be in here," Graham muttered. Then he turned a page and there it was.

The Castle on Deadman's Island, he read, *is one of several castles built in the Thousand Islands, on the border between the United States and Canada, by American captains of industry in the early 1900s.* This was followed by some statistics on the number of rooms (*53*), how many skilled tradesmen it took to build (*145*), and ended with *During the stock-market crash of 1929 and the Great Depression that followed, the castle changed hands several times. At the time of writing, it is vacant, as buyers of multimillion-dollar castles are hard to find during a depression.*

A bit out of date, Graham knew. For he was well aware that the castle had been bought in 1938 by Major Tripe, a wealthy Kingsportian who'd made his fortune prospecting for gold in Northern Ontario. But after only three summers enjoying his castle on the St. Lawrence, Major Tripe died there, suddenly, of an illness that baffled the doctors. "The curse of the castle," the locals said, nodding wisely.

The major had no immediate family and his will left all his assets to an animal shelter – except for the castle. Coveted by many Kingsportians, the castle was left to three of the major's friends to share jointly.

The major's present to his three friends would not have seemed unusual except that the three hated each other with a passion, as everyone in Kingsport knew. The major had always been a joker, and when his will was read, some people laughed and said this was his last practical joke.

Others, however, found the major's will appalling. Among these was Graham's mother. For one of the three new owners of the castle was her sister, Graham's aunt Henrietta.

"Practical joke, indeed!" Mrs. Graham had said to her husband at the dinner table when the news broke. "Mark my words, Alex, that will is going to lead to a heap of trouble. I just hope Henrietta isn't the one to suffer."

Her remark had aroused Graham's interest, leading him to the library to read up on the castle.

Now, having learned what he could, Graham reached up to slide the book back on the shelf. A piece of paper fell out and fluttered to the floor like a wounded bird. Curious, he picked it up and turned it over. There was a handwritten note.

Have important news about you-know-who. Urgent we act immediately. This is our chance. She suspects nothing. Meet me at the usual place – coal pile end. Tomorrow night at eight.

THREE

Graham read the note over several times. The ink looked fresh. It could have been written that very day.

As he was examining the note, he again got the feeling of being watched. He looked around quickly. Only two other people were in the reference room – a woman searching the stacks in the far corner and a man in a gray hat hurrying away.

He replaced the note and shelved the book. Not really his business if people wanted to swap notes in library books, like they were secret agents in a Hollywood spy movie. More likely, he thought, the note was written by some local guy – a rotter, as his mother would say – cheating on his wife and arranging a secret get-together with his girlfriend.

Back in the main library, Graham noticed the man in the gray hat he'd seen leaving the reference room. The man appeared to be absorbed in a newspaper.

Curious now, Graham turned away and strolled to the magazine rack. Then he wheeled around. Sure enough, the man was watching. His hooded eyes were leveled at him over the top of his newspaper.

The man rattled his paper and disappeared behind it again. Two can play at this game, Graham decided. He went out the front door of the library, waited a moment, then turned around and scooted back in. The man was already up and hurrying to the reference room. *Aha*, thought Graham.

He followed the bobbing gray fedora, keeping a row of metal shelves between himself and the wearer. Sure enough, the man took down the very book that Graham had been looking at – the book on castles.

As Graham watched, the man riffled through the pages until he found the note. He stood reading it, deep in thought. "So," Graham said to himself, "the note was meant for this man, not for someone's sweetheart." This was more than a romantic tryst. But what? He thought back to the note: *Urgent we act immediately. This is our chance.* Was he a Nazi spy?

He noted the man's stocky build, his confident stance, his chest thrown out, his loud green sports coat, yellow tie, and highly polished maroon brogues. Sharply dressed, though without any color sense whatsoever, more like a gangster than a spy. Not as Graham visualized a spy anyway, someone shifty and unobtrusive, keeping in the background, like, say, Peter Lorre in *The Maltese Falcon*, which he'd seen a few weeks ago at the Capitol Theater.

Besides, a Nazi spy in Kingsport was about as likely as a palm tree in the Arctic. Graham dismissed that idea. Who else, he wondered, would use a seldom-read book in the library as a safe place to pass notes back and forth? Bank robbers? Bootleggers? Smugglers? There had been a lot of the latter during Prohibition in the United States, smuggling whiskey across Lake Ontario.

Whoever it was, Graham did not want to get mixed up with them. He smiled to himself. What a shock the man in the gray fedora must have had when he saw someone else looking through that book, reading the note meant only for him.

But that was the end of it, as far as Graham was concerned. Nothing more than an amusing incident to tell his friend Neil, when they walked to school together in the morning.

It never occurred to Graham that the subject of the book – castles – could have anything to do with the note he'd found. Far-out speculation was for daydreamers – like Neil. Graham's mind dealt only in hard facts.

On the way home, Graham caught up with three girls from his high school, walking arm in arm, pleated knee-length skirts swinging, saddle shoes stepping in unison. He hesitated. He wanted to pass them, but he was awkward with girls – he couldn't seem to stop babbling in their presence. Still, he couldn't dawdle along at their pace either, or they'd think he was following them. One of them glanced back and said something to the other two, which made them giggle. Graham decided to cross the road.

Traffic was light – with the war and gas rationing, traffic in Kingsport was always light – and Graham was preoccupied with the piece he'd read in *Popular Mechanics* on the new technological marvel, television. He stepped blithely onto the road.

One of the girls screamed. Graham looked up and saw the grille of a car bearing down on him. He jumped back, felt a fender brush his hip and something whack him on the elbow. Then the car sped away in a flash of green. The driver was hunched over the wheel, his gray fedora pushed back, as the car dis-appeared around the corner, tires squealing.

Graham stood stunned. The road was now empty, and he wondered for a moment if he'd imagined the whole thing. The throb in his elbow told him he hadn't.

The girls clustered around him. "Are you all right, Graham?" one asked.

"Yes," he said. "Something hit me, though – the door handle or the mirror – right on the funny bone. My arm's all numb and tingly." He rubbed his elbow. "It's not the bone that causes the tingling sensation actually, it's the ulnar nerve. That's the nerve that runs down the arm and controls the third and fourth fingers of . . ." He stopped, seeing the girls glance at each other as if confirming that he really was weird.

"The car didn't even slow down," another girl said. "It swerved right at you. Good thing Jennie screamed."

"Thank you for alerting me," Graham said. "I wasn't paying attention. I was cogitating." Seeing them frown, he worried that they thought he'd used a dirty word.

The girls continued up the street, shaking their heads, while Graham, carefully looking both ways, crossed over and took the shortcut home through MacDonald Park.

It had been a strange day, he reflected. When he saw Neil in the morning, he'd tell him about finding the note in the library book and about the man trying to hide behind a newspaper while he spied on him. But he'd downplay his near miss with the car. Neil was too much of a worrier already.

FOUR

Neil waited until after school to make one last try to convince Graham that he should take his close call with the car more seriously.

"So what do you want me to do?" Graham said. "Run whenever I see a man in a gray fedora?"

"Look, the guy saw you reading the note meant for his eyes only," said Neil. "I figure he's worried that you've twigged to their scheme, whatever it is, and he can't take any chances."

"I suppose you could be right," Graham conceded.

"He's worried enough to try to eliminate you, or at

least scare you off. So whatever it is they're up to, it must be something shady."

Graham stopped to pick up a pebble, sparkling in the sunshine. "Sedimentary limestone," he said, examining it. "With embedded quartz crystals. Paleozoic era." He tucked the pebble in his pocket. "Anyway, don't worry, I can easily find out what he's up to. Then I'll know whether to take it seriously or not."

"How can you find out?"

"Simple. I'll eavesdrop on the meeting they arranged in that note. *'Meet me at the usual place – coal pile end,'* the note said. You know where that is, don't you?"

Neil's brow knitted. There were coal piles all over town – coal warmed Kingsport's homes and fueled its factories. "Ward's Coal, down by the bridge?" he guessed. He liked the slogan painted on the fence. He read it every time they went by in his father's old Ford: WARD KEEPS COAL, AND COAL KEEPS WARD.

"Ward's Coal?" Graham shook his head. "Unlikely. They'd be too conspicuous there. Think of a place where there are benches for people to sit and talk."

"I get it now," Neil said. "The waterfront!" It was his favorite place to go and watch the waves roll in. At the far end of the waterfront walkway was a dock where boats unloaded coal for the hospital power plant.

"Exactly," Graham said. "The perfect place for a rendezvous. They'd blend in and nobody would give them a second glance. Except yours truly. I shall just happen to be strolling by at eight o'clock tonight."

"You can't," Neil said.

Graham looked up sharply. "What do you mean? You've been urging me to take this seriously, and when I do . . ."

"I mean they know what you look like. One of them does, anyway – the guy who tried to run you down."

"I'll go in disguise then," Graham said. "Glue some bristles from my father's shaving brush on my lip, borrow his fedora, and –"

"Graham," Neil interrupted, "that's not good enough. Chances are the guy will still recognize you. Then he'll know he hasn't scared you off, and he'll really be after you. No, I'll go instead."

"You?"

"Sure. He won't suspect me. He's never seen me before."

Graham sneezed and dug out his handkerchief again. "Maybe you're right. No chance he'll mistake you for me, that's for sure." He looked up at his friend. "You're a good foot taller than shortie here and a lot thinner. But are you sure you want to get involved in this mess?"

"Of course I do – you've helped me often enough." Neil was thinking of their last detective venture together and of the countless times Graham had come to the rescue when he was stumped by some math problem. "I'll just saunter by, casual-like, and get a look at them. I may not be able to hear much of what they're saying, but at least we'll know who you have to watch out for. It'll be a cinch."

Actually, I'll be scared stiff, Neil thought, but I won't let Graham know that.

"It's starting to rain," Neil said. People strolling along the waterfront were opening umbrellas and picking up their pace. "Maybe they won't come."

"It's only sprinkling," Graham said. "They'll come." A few minutes later, he nudged Neil and pointed. "Must be them now, right on schedule."

Up ahead, two figures could be seen settling down on the last bench at the far end of the walkway. "Wait here," Neil said, and he set out alone.

As he neared the bench, Neil saw that one of the men wore the gray fedora and ugly green sports coat Graham had described. But the other, to Neil's surprise, was dressed in a dark blue suit. Graham had expected the second person might be a seedy criminal type, depending on how you interpreted the note. But this guy looked like a prosperous businessman, with his conservative clothes and furled umbrella.

The two men on the bench were arguing and gesticulating, but stopped as Neil approached. He glanced sideways at them as he went by. When he reached the end of the pavement, Neil turned and walked back, his hands in his pockets, whistling, which may have seemed odd behavior when it was getting dark and threatening rain. The two men looked up at him as he passed.

Neil hurried back to where Graham was waiting. "I heard some of what they said. They were arguing and the one said, 'But we can't go that far!' Then the one with the gray fedora said, 'Why the hell can't we? Serve her right.' They clammed up when I went by, but I got a good look at them and I know I've seen them before."

"You have? Where?"

"Not sure. I remember their pictures from somewhere. The newspaper, maybe." Neil stared at the darkening sky, trying to concentrate. "Something to do with a will . . ."

"Not Major Tripe's will?"

"Yeah, that's it!"

Graham slapped his forehead. "The major's will! Then it must be Grimsby and Snyder over there."

Neil wondered who they were and why Graham suddenly looked so concerned.

"You know, Major Tripe's castle was left to three people to share," Graham said. "It was in the paper."

"I guess I saw it, but I wasn't that interested. What's it got to do with some guy trying to run you down?" Neil stopped suddenly. "*Uh-oh*, look out. Here they come."

Busy talking, neither he nor Graham had noticed the two men get up from their bench and come towards them. It was too late to flee.

"Don't let them see you," Neil hissed. But there was no place to hide. Graham turned and pretended to be watching the waves.

One of the men stopped and stared at Graham's back. He said something to the other and nodded in Graham's direction. For a moment both men looked hard at him, then they walked on, their faces set.

FIVE

"So now will you tell me what this is all about?" Neil said. They were in his room, just back from their encounter on the waterfront. "Why are those guys out to get you?"

"In a nutshell," Graham said, "it's about money. And a man with a strange sense of humor who left his castle in the Thousand Islands to three people to share – three people who hate each other. One of the three is Jake Grimsby –"

"The guy with the gray fedora?"

"Right. The other is Carson Snyder –"

"The one who looks like a prosperous businessman?"

"Right again."

"But if they hate each other, why were they together?"

"That's what I'm worried about. Judging from what was in that note, they could be joining forces to get rid of the third person they're supposed to share the castle with."

"And who is that?"

"My aunt, Henrietta Stone. Aunt Etta, I call her."

"Your aunt! Then you'd better warn her."

Graham stood looking out the window at the rain slanting against the streetlight. "I would if I could."

"What d'you mean?"

"I mean Aunt Etta isn't here to warn. She told my mother that Grimsby and Snyder were both busy in town, so this was her chance to spend two weeks at the castle on her own. She's there now."

"Then phone her."

"There's no phone line to the island. Apparently, the major didn't intend to be bothered by phone calls from people wanting to drop in."

Isolated in a castle on an island, Neil could picture all sorts of grim things happening to Graham's aunt. But then he was always told he had an overactive imagination. "Where exactly is this castle?"

"On Deadman's Island."

"Deadman's! Isn't that the one that's supposed to be cursed?"

"Oh, that," Graham said. "It's just some superstition the locals have. The major didn't pay any attention to it when he bought the place, though I must admit he died there of a mysterious illness."

"I still think you should warn your aunt," Neil said. "Go there, if you can't phone. I'll come with you if you want."

"Easier said than done. We'd need a boat. Besides, Aunt Etta's a very independent person and she likes her privacy."

"Tell your folks, then. Maybe your dad would drive us downriver and help us find a boat."

Graham shook his head. "He'd never take us seriously – he'd say we were just playing Dick Tracy again. And it would only worry my mother. You know what my folks are like – the less said, the better."

"Then we'd better hope your aunt comes back to town soon."

"That's just it. She won't," Graham said. "She called my mother before she took off for the castle and said she's going on a long car trip afterwards."

"This gets worse and worse. A car trip where?"

"She wouldn't say. She said she was sick of all this

will business – her name in the paper and people giving her funny looks, laughing behind her back. When she leaves the castle, she's just going to get in her old Packard and drive south – she's been saving her gas coupons. She isn't sure when she'll come back, maybe not for a long time . . . until it all blows over."

"So if you don't get to her now, who knows when you'll see her again," Neil said.

"That's about the size of it, I'm afraid. Aunt Etta's always been able to take care of herself. I just hope she leaves before Grimsby and Snyder get there."

At Graham's house, his mother was concerned about Henrietta too. Not about Jake Grimsby or Carson Snyder harming her sister – that thought never occurred to her. After all, they were both well-known, though not well-liked, businessmen. Her concern was that the two would somehow manage to cheat Henrietta out of her rightful share.

As head of the Historical Society, Henrietta clashed regularly with Grimsby and Snyder over the preservation of Kingsport's old limestone buildings. Snyder, a real-estate agent known for sharp dealings, wanted to sell them to the highest bidder. Grimsby, a slum landlord, wanted to buy them cheap to add to his string of rundown rooming houses.

And now these three were to share a castle in the Thousand Islands! The major even put in a clause stating that the castle was not to be sold, and if it was, the entire proceeds would revert to the animal shelter. Nor could an owner's share be passed on to his heirs. On an owner's death, his or her shares would revert to the other surviving owners. The major, who got along with everybody, apparently wanted his three friends to see the error of their ways and learn to tolerate each other.

"But Henrietta absolutely cannot stand either of those two men," Graham's mother said. "And that Barbara Snyder's even worse than her husband, Carson. She seems to think the castle is all hers, Henrietta says.

"It's not funny either, Alex," she added. For Graham's father couldn't help chuckling.

"Well, Henrietta doesn't *have* to go there, does she?" he said. "If she just stays away, then she'll never have to deal with those two devious rascals, as she calls them."

"It's not that simple, Alex. There's upkeep and staff to deal with. You can't just leave a castle worth millions to go to ruin."

"Then let the other two handle it."

"And do what they want with it? Those two? You know Henrietta would never allow that."

"No, I suppose not. But I wouldn't worry. Your sister can look after herself. Henrietta isn't called the tiny dynamo for nothing."

Mrs. Graham sighed. "I know, but I don't trust those two men."

SIX

The following week was the best of times for the students of Kingsport High – the start of the summer holidays.

For Neil, the end of school also brought his girl-friend, Crescent, home from Havergal College, a private school in Toronto. Now, however, Crescent was into sailing and spent most of her days at the Kingsport Yacht Club, where she raced her family's sailing dinghy. They often got together in the evenings – not often enough for Neil, though.

In the meantime, he and Graham were thinking about finding summer jobs to make some pocket money. It was Neil's idea, for Graham would have been quite content to spend most of his summer at the library.

"I want a job where I can make some real money," Neil said.

"You've got your paper route," Graham reminded him.

"That's peanuts," Neil said. He felt a little guilty, remembering how excited he'd been to get the paper route a few years back, when jobs of any kind were scarce. Now, in the third year of the war, jobs were easy to come by as so many men left to join up.

They were in Graham's room, Neil searching the HELP WANTED ads in the *Evening Standard*. "'Pin boys wanted for bowling alley,'" he read out.

Graham shuddered. "Thanks, but no thanks."

"'Thirty-five cents a hour!'"

Graham wasn't impressed. "Danger pay. You're down there in a pit, dodging flying pins and hurtling balls, with potbellied bowlers shouting at you to hurry up."

"Well, how about this then? 'Delivery boys. Must have bicycle with carrier.' Or this: 'Grocery store helpers, bag packing and carry out, twenty-five cents an hour plus tips.'"

"I suppose," Graham said. "Monetarily rewarding, but not very stimulating."

"It's the best we can do, Graham. If we were a few years older, we could make sixty cents an hour working shifts at the aluminum plant. Imagine, sixty cents an hour!" Neil pictured the money piling up in his bank account – it would make him feel good and safe. He'd seen too many hoboes begging at the door for a meal during the Great Depression. He never wanted to find himself in a fix like that.

But Graham, he knew, was different. Science, physics, math – these mattered more to Graham than money. Neil knew he'd have trouble interesting him in a job, but he needed Graham with him. For Graham had confidence and the gift of the gab – things Neil himself lacked.

"I think I'll try for one of those helper jobs at Wheatley's grocery tomorrow," Neil said. "Coming with me?"

Graham looked up from the pad he'd been doodling numbers on, solving quadratic equations just for fun. "Where?"

"To Wheatley's, of course. Why not give it a try – what have you got to lose? If you don't like it, you can always leave. We'll go see them in the morning, okay?"

Graham sighed. "I suppose."

They turned onto the main street, passing a row of old office buildings with alleyways in between. Ahead, in the next block, sat Wheatley's, Purveyors of Fine Groceries. Neil hitched up his pants and ran a finger around under his shirt collar, where it pinched. He hadn't worn a tie since the class picture, and it felt like he was choking. Graham, he noticed, hadn't bothered with a tie, but at least his pants had a crease of sorts, as if he'd put them under the mattress the night before.

Beside him, Graham stopped suddenly. "Hey," he said. "There it is!"

"Yeah, Wheatley's. Up ahead. I know."

"No, not the store, the car." Graham was staring at a new, dark green Studebaker parked in front of the building they were passing. "Same grille – looks like a shark's snout. I remember looking up and seeing it coming right at me."

"That's the car that almost hit you?"

Graham nodded. "Unless there's two new, dark green Studebakers in town."

The car was parked in front of a building that was three stories high and made of limestone blocks with their characteristic rough-textured look. Like the dour Scottish stonemasons who had constructed many of Kingsport's buildings, it was plain with no fancy trimmings, but rock solid.

"Maybe the guy who owns the car has an office in there," Neil said.

"Could be. Wait here, I'll take a look. If Jake Grimsby's office is there, I'll know for sure he was the one who tried to run me down."

Inside the door, a glass-fronted board listed the building's occupants. Graham ran down the list of names, stopping at one. *J.K. Grimsby*, it read. *Suite 303*.

The door from the street opened and someone brushed past him. Footsteps hurried up the stairs, then paused partway up. Graham averted his face and the footsteps continued, until the sound of them died away. Somewhere above, a door slammed.

"His office is in there, all right," Graham said, when he was back on the pavement. "Third floor."

Neil automatically looked up. A face appeared at a third-floor window, screened by a pot of red geraniums on the windowsill. "The guy who just went in might have been Grimsby," he said. "I'm pretty sure he was at the waterfront last week. Think he could have recognized you?"

"Cripes, I hope not."

"Hey, we'd better get going, or we'll be late for the interview at Wheatley's," Neil said. He started to move away.

But Graham was staring at the car again.

"The man said to be there at ten," Neil insisted. "C'mon."

Graham sighed. "Nothing I can do here, I guess." He took one step forward, just as a heavy flowerpot hurtled downward, crashing to the sidewalk behind him.

"*What?*" Graham turned and stared at the jumble of clay, black earth, and broken red geraniums, inches from his back foot. "Where the devil did *that* come from?"

Neil turned. "Holy hell, Graham! If you hadn't moved when you did . . ."

"Precisely. And I'll bet it wasn't any accident." His head back, Graham eyed the windows above. "I'd estimate from its trajectory that it came from the third window from the left on the top floor."

"Hey, where you going? Our job interview –"

SEVEN

—

Graham yanked open the door of the building. "You go for the interview. I want to find out if that window belongs to suite number 303. If it does, then this is serious."

"Wait. What if Grimsby sees you?"

"So? You think he's going to pull a gun and shoot me down in cold blood? No, not our friend Grimsby. His modus operandi, I see now, is to make it look like an accident. First the car, then this." He disappeared inside.

Neil was torn – go now, or stay in case Graham needed help and be late for the job interview. He stayed.

As the minutes ticked by, he became increasingly uneasy. Finally he went inside and mounted the stairs.

Reaching the third floor, Neil found the hallway empty. The sound of voices and the clackety-clack of typewriters came and went as he passed each door, noting the names on the glass: *301, Lloyd Woods, Attorney-at-Law; 302, Fred E. Pennyfeather, Tax Accountant; 303, J.S. Grimsby, Property Management.*

He stopped and listened at the door of 303. He heard a man's voice, but couldn't make out what he was saying. Just then Graham popped out of the next office. He motioned silently to Neil, then he ducked back in. Neil joined him.

The office was empty, except for cans of paint, brushes, and drop cloths scattered about. Graham was leaning against the wall separating the office from the adjoining one, which was Grimsby's. He was holding one end of a drinking glass, with his ear pressed to the other end. He signaled to Neil, putting his finger to his lips.

Neil waited. He heard a door shut at the far end of the hall. He pushed the office door closed as footsteps approached, passed, and faded away.

When Graham touched his arm, he jumped. "Time to vamoose," Graham whispered, "before the painters come back from their break."

"Could you hear what Grimsby was saying?" Neil asked, when they were on the sidewalk again.

Graham nodded. "Some of it – once I found the glass in the washroom. An empty glass, as you may know, amplifies the sounds coming through a wall. Sound waves are conducted by –"

"Never mind the physics lesson," Neil interrupted. "What was he saying?"

"He was on the phone to someone – Snyder, I suspect. I only heard the end of it, but it didn't sound good. I'm afraid they're out to get her all right."

"Your aunt? How?"

"He didn't go into that. But they're definitely going to the castle."

"When?"

"I didn't hear that either. Not soon, I hope. Somehow I've got to get to the island ahead of them and warn Aunt Etta."

"We," Neil said. "*We* have to get there."

"I thought you were going for that job at Wheatley's."

"Someone's got to keep you out of trouble. I'll go see the man at Wheatley's now and tell him I can't start right away."

"Great. Two heads are better than one. Now all we have to do is figure out some way to get there."

"I have an idea about that."

"Shoot."

"Crescent's family has rented a cottage down the river. We could hitchhike that far and ask her to take us to Deadman's Island in their boat."

"You mean row all the way?"

"No, no, it's a sailboat. It's at the yacht club now, but her family is going to trailer it to the cottage. Crescent's a good sailor, maybe she'll take us to the island. I can ask her anyway. I'll go see her today."

"That would be our answer all right, if Crescent's willing. Good thing she's nuts about you."

"I wish," Neil said.

EIGHT

Crescent Savage headed her dinghy straight at the dock and hauled in the mainsail. The boat forged ahead and a high-speed collision seemed imminent. She waited coolly until the bow was within a few feet of the dock, then shoved the tiller sharply to starboard.

The dinghy swung into the wind, the jib and mainsail flapped noisily, and *Discovery* glided smoothly alongside the dock, where Neil was shifting uncomfortably from one foot to the other.

He'd been there only once before, when Crescent had taken him sailing. His family wasn't part of the yacht club set and he felt out of place, like a hobo at a garden party.

Neil reached down to grab the bow line while Crescent dropped the sails. The mad luffing of the sails ceased, and again it was a quiet summer afternoon at the Kingsport Yacht Club.

"Hi, Neil," Crescent said. "Saw you waving. What's up?"

"Didn't mean to spoil your sail," he said. "You were really going out there." Now that he was here, he wondered if asking her to take them to the castle wouldn't be too much. He had no idea how far away it was – he just knew that the castle was down the river from her family's cottage. They might even have to camp somewhere overnight, if they couldn't make it there and back in a day.

He pictured sitting around a campfire with Crescent, listening to waves breaking on a rocky shore and the whispering of wind in the pines, and gazing up at a million stars. Of course Graham would be there too, talking nonstop, so they probably wouldn't hear waves or wind in the pines. Still . . .

"I wanted to ask you a favor," he said. "A big favor –"

"Hey, Crescent, nice breeze out there today," a voice called. Neil turned and saw a tanned blond guy, in a bathing suit and T-shirt, rigging a brightly varnished dinghy in a nearby slip. He looked about his age, but Neil didn't recognize him.

The guy sauntered over and looked down at Crescent, who was holding onto the dock to keep the dinghy from banging. "Race you around the buoys," he said.

Neil felt a surge of jealousy.

"Not right now, Tom – maybe later," Crescent said. "You two know each other?"

Neil forced a smile and stuck out his hand. "Neil Graves," he said. "Good to meet you."

"Tom Snyder," the guy said, giving him the once-over. Ignoring Neil's extended hand, he turned and strolled back to his boat.

Neil burned. Tom Snyder had managed to make him feel like an awkward outsider. *You don't belong here*, Tom's look had said.

"We can talk later if you like," Neil said to Crescent.

"Oh, Tom can wait. He's always after me to race. His father bought that new dinghy this year because their old one wasn't fast enough for him."

Suddenly the last name struck Neil – *Snyder*. "Is Tom's father Carson Snyder?"

"That's him. I met Tom last winter. He's at Upper Canada, which isn't far from Havergal."

Neil's face fell. He pictured Tom and Crescent together at school dances, dancing cheek to cheek. All he wanted to do now was get away from this place, where he, unlike Crescent and Tom Snyder, didn't belong.

Crescent must have sensed his unease. "Stick around," she said. "It's all right, you're my guest."

"I have to go," he hedged. "How about tonight?"

"Sure, Neil," Crescent said. "I'd love to. What time?"

"Around seven?"

She smiled up at him. "Okay. We could go for a walk while you tell me what this mysterious favor is all about."

"Once around the course, Crescent," Tom said, coming up behind them. "I'll give you a thirty-second head start."

Neil walked away quickly, past the clubhouse and out the gate. Swinging shut behind him, the gate gave him a bump in the rear, as if sending him on his way. He almost turned around and kicked it.

NINE

—

Neil and Crescent bicycled to Outlet Park and walked down to the water, but it was crowded with soldiers and their girlfriends, so they climbed a fence and took the path into the woods. Crescent wore a wooly sweater against the evening chill. The beige turtleneck Neil liked, the one she had on the first time he saw her.

"This park was empty before the army camp was built," he said. "We often came here when I was with the Boy Scouts." It was only a few years ago. How things change, Neil thought. His scout leader had joined the air force when the war broke out, and the troop had never been the same.

"I know," Crescent said. "I vaguely remember Dad bringing me here when I was four, or maybe five. There were only a few hoboes here then, trying to avoid the cops and find a place to sleep."

They came to a stream and crossed it with a leap. "This favor," Neil began. He stopped and looked at her. "If it's too much to ask, I'll understand."

Crescent smiled. "Oh, Neil, you'd never make a salesman."

He blushed. "The thing is, Graham and I really need your help."

She shrugged. "Well, sure I'll help, if I can. But don't tell me you two are in the detective business again."

"You guessed it. Not that we want to be. But let me tell you what happened to Graham. Because it's left us no choice."

Crescent listened attentively while he told her about the major's will. It was familiar to her from the accounts in the paper, but she looked startled when he described Graham's two near "accidents." "Is Mr. Grimsby that ruthless?" she asked dubiously.

"He sure tried to get rid of Graham. So how far would he go to have his aunt out of the way? And Mr. Snyder's in cahoots with him. They'd take over her share of the castle."

"But Mr. Grimsby and Mr. Snyder dislike each other as much as they dislike Henrietta Stone," Crescent said. "You only have to read about one of the council meetings to know that."

Neil nodded. "I know, and I don't quite understand why they're working together now. But Graham's convinced they've joined forces against his aunt and I think he's right. We need to warn her, but she's on the island where there's no phone, and we have no way to get there. How far is the castle from your cottage anyway?"

"An hour or two by sailboat, depending on the wind. You go downriver five miles or so, then cross the shipping channel to Deadman's Island."

Neil waited. It was up to Crescent. He wasn't the type to push her to take them there.

"That boy will never make it in business," he once overheard his father say to his mother. "Sometimes you gotta be pushy. If I gave in every time someone complained about my bill, I'd never make a dime." Neil's father's plumbing business had teetered on the brink of bankruptcy during the Great Depression, but was prospering again with the army-camp construction contract.

"Give him time," his mother had said. "He'll find himself."

Neil wasn't sure what she meant by that. He was the way he was.

"I'll take you, if you want," Crescent said. "I'd like to explore that part of the river."

"Great!" Neil replied. "We'll hitchhike to your place. Whenever you say."

"We're leaving tomorrow. We'll be there for a few weeks, so come anytime."

"Would it be okay with your folks? Using the boat, I mean."

"You know Dad. Easygoing."

He noticed she didn't say that about her mother. Maggie Savage was more intense, as Neil knew, but she'd always treated him well.

The path veered around a fallen beech tree. It was bench height and practically invited you to stay and enjoy the quiet of the woods. They sat on the fallen tree and he put his arm around her. Crescent laid her head on his shoulder and he inhaled her scent. She lifted her face and nibbled his neck. He was content.

"Neil?"

"Yes."

"Why do you only . . ."

"What is it?"

"Why don't you . . . oh, to heck with talking." She reached up, pulled his head down, and fastened her lips against his. They stayed that way for a while.

"*Umm*, that was nice," Neil said, which didn't half describe the rush he got from her soft warm lips.

— 45 —

Crescent sighed. "I'll say. Why don't we do it more often? Why do we only kiss when we're saying good night after a date?"

Neil looked away. "I guess I . . . well, I wasn't sure you would want me to . . . you know, be after you all the time."

"Try me," Crescent said, and snuggled in his arms.

Above them, a pair of gray squirrels chased each other round and round a tree, until it was hard to tell who was chasing whom.

TEN

Neil was packing spare socks, underwear, and a toothbrush in his knapsack when his mother came into the room. "This camping trip you're going on," she said, "where exactly are you staying?"

"Not sure till we get there," Neil said, wondering if one pair of socks was enough, or whether to bother with socks at all. "There's lots of campsites in the Thousand Islands. There's even one near Crescent's cottage."

"Maybe Graham's aunt will invite you to stay with her."

"I doubt it. Graham says she likes her privacy." Neil had been deliberately vague about the purpose of their expedition, not wanting to worry his mother. "Just a few days camping," he'd said. "Great weather for it. Crescent's going to show us the Thousand Islands in her boat, and while we're at it, Graham wants to see his aunt's castle."

"Well, if his aunt does ask you to stay there, you boys make yourselves useful," his mother instructed. "Don't expect to be waited on. And don't forget to thank her."

He threw a T-shirt into the knapsack. "No, Mom, we won't."

"You'd better take a blanket. You can have that old army blanket of your grandfather's. It still gets cold at night. And what are you taking to eat?"

He stuffed his envelope of paper-route money into the pocket of the knapsack. "There's stores there, Mom."

"Hot dogs and potato chips and chocolate bars, I suppose. Well, I guess it won't kill you for a few days. When will you be back?"

"Depends. If it stays hot, why rush back to town?"

"Is there a phone at the cottage Crescent's family has rented?"

"I doubt it." Neil zipped up his knapsack. "Don't worry about us, Mom. We'll be okay."

His mother sighed. "Well, you be careful, Neil."

"Sure, Mom." He headed for the door.

"And don't forget the blanket – it's in the spare room."

"Okay. Bye then. See you when we get back."

At the window, his mother watched him walk up the street until he disappeared around the corner.

"Kids these days," she said to her husband at dinner. "Independent as all get out."

Neil's father wasn't really listening. Not that he wasn't concerned about his son's welfare, but his mind was on the rush job he had at the new army hospital. More and more Canadian war casualties were being repatriated – bombers were over Germany almost every night now, many of them manned by Canadian aircrews, and the Desert War in North Africa was heating up. Neil's father was behind schedule on the work and couldn't find experienced plumbers at any price.

"Half the time, I don't know where he is," Neil's mother continued. "Now he's off on some camping trip with Graham. George . . . George, do you hear me?"

Mr. Graves looked up. "It's the war," he said. "Kids know they could be in the army overseas in a few years."

Mrs. Graves shuddered. "I just hope the war's over before Neil's old enough. If I know him, he'll sign up on his eighteenth birthday."

The first half hour was smooth sailing. Crescent handled the tiller and the mainsail while Neil tended the jib, hauling it in or out as she directed. Soon, he began to get the hang of it.

You let the jib out until it starts to flap, he realized, then pull it in until it stops – not too much though, just enough, so that it makes a nice smooth curve, matching the curve of the main. Then the two sails work together, pulling *Discovery* along at a fast clip.

It was downwind all the way – a broad reach, Crescent called it – with the wind on their stern quarter. They barreled along. But then the wind shifted so that it was dead astern, and the jib, now blanketed by the main, sagged like an old sock. The boat slowed.

Crescent showed Neil how to push the jib out to the other side, so the main was on one side and the jib on the other. Wing and wing, she said it was called. *Discovery* immediately picked up speed again.

Graham simply tried to stay out of the way. When the wind freshened and the dinghy heeled sharply in a gust, he grabbed for support. "*Uh-oh*, are we going to tip?"

Crescent assured him that heeling was normal, and she eased the mainsail out to spill some wind and settle the dinghy down.

They were sailing along the north shore of the St. Lawrence River, and islands were streaming by. Large islands, small islands, islands dense with tall pines, islands with one lone pine, islands with sprawling mansions, islands with one-room cabins, and islands with nothing but granite rock. There were two tiny islands connected by a little arched wooden bridge, like a miniature of the big suspension bridge connecting Canada and the United States – the Thousand Islands Bridge opened jointly by President Roosevelt and Prime Minister Mackenzie King in 1938.

"Interesting rock formations," Graham said, as he watched the islands pass. "Mostly igneous. Precambrian period. Formed several billion years ago. Much older than the limestone you find around Kingsport – it's only five hundred million years old."

Only five hundred million years, Neil thought. "Do you suppose there really are a thousand islands?"

"Actually 1,864," Graham said. "I looked it up. Some on the Canadian side, some on the American."

Occasionally, one of the familiar red freighters, long and slim, steamed by in the ship channel, going downriver to Montreal or upriver to Lake Ontario. As long as a football field, they had to be slim to go through the locks that bypassed the Long Sault Rapids. There was talk of building a seaway that would flood the rapids and allow ocean freighters into Lake Ontario, but all that was put aside in the struggle to win the war.

"We must be getting close," Crescent said. She bent over her chart. When she straightened up, she pointed across the river to the south.

"Deadman's Island should be right over there," she said. "We have to cross the ship channel first. Haul in on the jib sheet, Neil." She changed course to head south, and then they were sailing across the wind, the dinghy bounding over the waves.

Graham had gone unusually quiet. He was looking pale.

"Are you all right, Graham?" Crescent asked.

"Bit queasy," he said, in a weak voice. "A touch of mal de mer, I'm afraid."

"Don't look at the scenery," Crescent said. "That's the worst thing for seasickness. Look straight ahead. Watch the sails."

Graham kept his eyes on the sails. But being Graham, he didn't just watch them, he studied them. "The way the mainsail curves reminds me of an air-plane wing," he said, pointing to the front edge of the main, where it was attached to the mast. "Same principle, I assume. It's pulling the boat along like an

airplane wing lifts a plane. It's Bernoulli's Principle –
you know, air flowing over a venturi creates a vacuum
that pulls –"

"Sorry to interrupt," Crescent said, "but there it is
ahead. Deadman's Island."

"That one?" Neil said. For the island they were
approaching had only pine trees and one cottage on it,
as far as he could see.

"No, the big island behind it."

Then, as they rounded the point, the castle leaped
out at them, dwarfing its surroundings. It dominated
the blue water, the granite rocks, and even the stately
pines.

"Great balls of fire!" Graham said, gazing up at it.
"A perfect setting for *Macbeth*!"

ELEVEN

The myriad windows of the castle stared down at the little dinghy scornfully, as if daring it to come closer.

"Six chimneys, at least," Neil said, counting those he could see. "And three or four roof peaks. What a pile!"

Crescent turned the boat into the wind and they glided past a huge boathouse – a smaller version of the castle, like the offspring of a giant.

"'The rich man in his castle,'" Graham quoted the poet Cecil Frances Alexander, "'the poor man at his gate.'"

"Not much doubt which we are," Neil said.

At the dock, a large sign greeted them: PRIVATE PROPERTY – POSITIVELY NO TRESPASSING. Underneath the red lettering was a black skull and crossbones. The major had liked his privacy.

When they landed, no one appeared. The gravelly cawing of a raven was the only sound that broke the silence. "At least the castle doesn't have a drawbridge to keep us out," Graham said. They dropped the sails, tied *Discovery* securely, and headed up the hill to the castle.

Walking up the path, the sweet smell of juniper lured them on. The castle's marble steps led to an immense wooden door, with a heavy knocker in the form of a snarling lion's head. Just like the lion that signaled the start of MGM movies, Neil thought.

Graham knocked. They waited.

As he reached to knock again, the heavy door swung open and they were confronted by a stout formidable woman with a duster in her hand. She frowned and looked past them to where their boat was docked.

"You're not allowed to dock here, you kids," she said. "This is private property."

"It's all right, ma'am, I'm –" Graham began.

"Go dock over there, on Lovesick Island." The woman gestured with her chin to another island nearby. "It's public and there are campsites there." She started to close the door.

"But I'm here to see my aunt," Graham said quickly. "Henrietta Stone. I'm her nephew."

The woman turned back. "Well, why didn't you say so?"

Graham resisted the urge to say he couldn't get a word in. He waited for her to invite them in, but she continued to block the doorway, her arms crossed in front of her ample bosom. "Miss Stone's not here."

"But she told my mother she would be staying for two weeks. That was just last week."

"Oh, she was here all right, but then she left."

"When was that, exactly?"

The woman gave him an exasperated look, making it plain that she wasn't about to stand here answering his impertinent questions, even if he was the nephew of one of the new owners. That was when Crescent stepped in.

"We're sorry to trouble you," she said, "but it's important, Mrs. . . . *uh*."

"Ruff. Ruby Ruff," the woman said, turning her gaze on Crescent.

"I know you must have a lot to do, Mrs. Ruff, looking after this magnificent place," Crescent said, "but we'd really appreciate your help."

The woman's look softened. "Better come in then," she said gruffly. "Can't talk on the doorstep."

She led them down a wide marble-tiled hallway, past a sweeping staircase that could have come out of a 1930s Hollywood musical, to a kitchen the size of a small school gym.

"Don't see how I can help you much," she said, sitting them down at a massive wooden table. Ignoring the boys, she addressed her remarks to Crescent. "All I know is, Miss Stone came last week and she was still here Saturday when they showed up unannounced."

"When who showed up?"

"Why, the other new owners, Mr. Grimsby and Mr. Snyder, of course."

Graham and Neil exchanged startled glances.

TWELVE

—

"They showed up on Saturday!" Graham exclaimed.

Mrs. Ruff turned to Graham like he was some dimwit. "That's what I said, didn't I? Your aunt seemed surprised to see them too."

"I guess she would be," Graham said. "According to my mother, she came because neither Grimsby nor Snyder would be here and she would have the place to herself."

"Did they tell you they were coming, Mrs. Ruff?" Crescent asked.

"They never tell me anything, those two. Just arrived in a fancy speedboat they rented from Muldoon's

Marina over on the shore. The peculiar thing was, they came together. They usually fight like alley cats, if they're here at the same time. And if all four are here, it's even worse. It doesn't happen often, thank goodness."

"Four? There are three owners, aren't there?" Graham said.

Mrs. Ruff gave him a withering look. "I was referring to your aunt, Mr. Grimsby, Mr. Snyder, *and* Mrs. Snyder. That's four, isn't it? And Mrs. Snyder is the worst of the lot. She acts like the queen of the castle, that one. Thinks she should have it all to herself, I said to my Leonard, and expects her husband to get it for her."

"Another Lady Macbeth," Graham remarked, "egging her husband on."

Mrs. Ruff frowned at him. "Lady Macbeth! You hard of hearing? I said Snyder, not Macbeth. And she's no lady, the way she leads that husband of hers around by the nose."

The back door to the kitchen opened and a pale scrawny man in overalls shambled in. He stopped uncertainly when he saw them.

"Have you finished trimming the hedges yet, Leonard?" Mrs. Ruff demanded.

"Not yet. There's miles of them, Ruby," he protested. "How about some lunch?"

"Later. Can't you see I've got visitors? Go try fixing that outboard."

"My husband," she said, when Leonard shuffled out again, grumbling. "He brings me over in the boat every morning. Sometimes he stays to look after the gardening. Now, where were we, dear?"

"You were telling us about the others arriving," Crescent prompted.

"Oh, yes. Well, they had quite a set-to with Miss Stone. I could hear the shouting from the kitchen. Miss Stone may be a small woman, but she stands right up to those big men. She said they had no right to barge in here without telling her. Snyder said they would come any time it suited them. Then Miss Stone said she couldn't stand being here with them and if they didn't leave, she would. 'Suits us,' Grimsby said, 'the sooner the better.'"

"And when did she leave?" Graham asked anxiously.

But Mrs. Ruff wasn't going to be hurried with her story. "By then it was almost time for me to go, so I made a casserole and put it in the oven for them. 'Glad I don't have to stay and listen to any more of that,' I said to Leonard. I was feeling sorry for poor Miss Stone. But then, just as I was leaving, Snyder told me that something had come up and he and Grimsby would have to go back to Kingsport the next day. I thought, thank the Lord I won't be putting up with those two all next week. It's no picnic when they're here, I can tell you."

"I'm sure it isn't," Crescent said, doing her best to keep Mrs. Ruff talking.

"So I said to Leonard, 'That's a relief – they're leaving. And Miss Stone must be relieved too. Now she won't have to go.'" Mrs. Ruff paused. "But I guess she left anyway."

"You guess?"

"Well, she wasn't here when I came back Monday morning – Sunday's my day off. The place was quiet as a tomb."

"No sign of her?" Graham asked.

Mrs. Ruff ignored him. "At first I thought Miss Stone must be having her morning swim. She's some swimmer, that one. Twice around the island every morning, rain or shine. She reminds me of that famous swimmer everybody was talking about a few years back. You know, the one at the New York World's Fair in 1939. Eleanor something . . ." Clearly Ruby Ruff liked having someone to gossip with, other than Leonard.

"Eleanor Holm, you mean?" Crescent said. "She's a champion swimmer and a movie star too."

"That's the one. Eleanor Holm. Anyway, when she didn't show up later – Miss Stone, I mean, not Eleanor Holm – I went up to her bedroom and saw that her suitcase was gone and most of her clothes. Then I looked in the boathouse and saw that her boat was gone too – she'd bought a runabout to use when she was here. So I knew Miss Stone must have decided to go away after all. Funny though, she didn't leave a note. She's usually pretty good about letting me know her comings and goings."

"So you've no idea where she went?"

Mrs. Ruff shook her head. "Just what she told me the day she arrived – when she left here in two weeks, she was going on a long trip. Said she wanted to get away from Kingsport and she'd just keep driving till she found somewhere nice to stay."

"But why would she leave so soon? Grimsby and Snyder were going," Graham put in.

Mrs. Ruff kept on talking to Crescent as if Graham were invisible. "So I guess we'll see her when we see her," she said, "and who knows when that will be."

"I don't believe a word of it," Graham said.

That remark finally got Mrs. Ruff's attention. She turned to him, bristling. "How dare you! I won't be accused of lying by a young pup still wet behind the ears. I'm a respectable, churchgoing wife and mother." She got up and seized a heavy cast-iron frying pan.

Graham prepared to duck, until he saw her slam the frying pan down on the stove.

"I'm sure Graham didn't mean it that way, Mrs. Ruff," Crescent said quickly.

"*Humph*," Mrs. Ruff said, and she snatched a can of beans from the cupboard and a carton of eggs from the fridge.

"You misinterpreted me, Mrs. Ruff," Graham said. "Let me rephrase my remark. I don't believe it likely that my aunt just suddenly upped and drove away, when she'd only been here a week. She isn't like that. She's very deliberate, and when she decides what she's going to do, she sticks to it. No, Mrs. Ruff, I have reason to doubt she ever left. Something must have happened to her while she was here."

"What could possibly happen to her here?" Mrs. Ruff snorted, cracking three eggs into the pan.

"Has anyone checked to see if her car is still where she parked it?" Graham said.

Mrs. Ruff smiled triumphantly. "First thing I thought of, when I got home on Monday. I called Muldoon's Marina, where she leaves it, and Clarence Muldoon said her car was gone when he got in on Monday morning. Now, if you'll excuse me," she said frostily, "I have to fry up something for Leonard's lunch, if I want him to keep working."

Crescent and Neil got up to leave, but Graham, they could see, was set to continue quizzing Mrs. Ruff.

"Not now," Neil said quietly, and he jerked his head toward the door.

"What did you do that for?" Graham said outside. "There's more I need to find out. I was just getting warmed up."

"So was Mrs. Ruff," Neil said. "Not only warmed up, but steamed up. You're not going to get any more out of her today."

"It's time to start back anyway," Crescent said. "I told Mom and Dad we'd be back before dark."

Graham protested. "But what about Aunt Etta?"

"I'm sorry, Graham, but we've got a long sail against the wind. If we don't show up, they'll have everyone out looking for us."

At the dock, Crescent got in and prepared to raise the sails, while Neil uncleated the lines. Graham, however, remained on the dock, looking back at the castle, frowning.

"I'm not going," he said.

THIRTEEN

Neil and Crescent looked at Graham in astonishment. "It's all right," he said. "You guys go ahead. I'm staying here."

"But, Graham, Mrs. Ruff won't let you stay here," Crescent said.

"That's for sure. Not if she knows," Graham agreed. "She took an instant dislike to me . . . I don't know why – I mean, all I did was ask her a few simple questions. I'll keep out of sight until she goes home. The thing is, I have a feeling something happened to Aunt Etta when Grimsby and Snyder were here, and I can't shake it. I hope I'm wrong, but I'm not leaving until I find out."

"But Mrs. Ruff said your aunt's boat was gone," Neil said. "And the man at the marina told her the car was gone too, so it seems she must have left on her trip."

"Possibly," Graham said, "or else someone wanted to make it look like she'd left. A boat can easily disappear – all you'd have to do is untie it and let it drift away. A car can be made to disappear too. As soon as Mrs. Ruff said that Grimsby and Snyder had shown up here unexpectedly, I thought *uh-oh*. I've got this creepy feeling about last Sunday, when Aunt Etta was here alone with those two. If anything did happen to her, there could be clues somewhere in the castle."

Neil was torn. He'd looked forward to sailing back with Crescent, yet he wanted to help his friend. "I don't know what you've got in mind, Graham," he said, "but I'll stay if you need me."

Graham looked relieved. "I must say, I wasn't exactly looking forward to searching the castle by myself after dark. I'm the first to admit that I'm not the bravest of souls."

Neil put his hand on Crescent's arm. "If I stay, you'll have to sail back alone. Do you mind?"

"It's all right," she said, but he could hear the disappointment in her voice. "I'm used to single-handing.

You stay and help Graham. But where will you sleep, and what will you do about food?"

"Here's my plan," Graham said. . . .

They made a great show of embarking, Crescent calling, "Coming about!" in a loud voice as she tacked back and forth in front of the dock, more than necessary.

Beside her in the cockpit, Neil and Graham made themselves conspicuous, to be sure Leonard, who was in the boathouse fiddling with the outboard, saw the three of them leaving.

They cleared the island and turned south to circle it, keeping their eyes peeled for a place to land on the far side. There were no beaches; the most promising place was a sheltered cove with a rocky shore. They dropped the sails there, pulled up the centerboard, and paddled silently in until they were close enough for Neil and Graham to wade the rest of the way, sneakers in hand.

A smooth gray rock, humped like an elephant's back, sloped down to the water's edge. They scrambled up it, then turned and waved as Crescent raised the sails. She was soon out of sight around the end of the island. She'd agreed to come back in the morning to pick them up at the same spot. "And bring something for breakfast, please," Graham said.

Now, Neil and Graham sat on the rock in the sun, waiting. There was nothing to do but keep out of sight until they heard the Ruffs' outboard start up.

The afternoon passed slowly. Once they heard a voice and hid in the bushes, but it was only Mrs. Ruff calling Leonard. Neil remained watchful, and Graham fell asleep. A chipmunk crept out of hiding and skittered across his chest. From the top of a swaying pine, the raven called to them with one of his many voices, letting them know that he was aware they were still on his island.

Finally, Neil heard the outboard starting up. He waited until its sound faded into the distance, then he shook Graham. "They're gone," he said.

Graham got to his feet groggily. "I'm glad you woke me. I dreamt I met Frankenstein in the cellar and he was about to throttle me."

They approached the back entrance to the castle cautiously. When they'd been in the kitchen earlier with Mrs. Ruff, Graham had taken note of the lock on the back door. "A cinch to jimmy," Neil had said later, when Graham described it to him. "There's one of those on our back door at home. I can open it easy."

Neil got out his penknife. It was only a matter of a few minutes fiddling and they were in.

They stood in the middle of the empty kitchen and looked around. In the absolute silence that surrounded them, Neil grew apprehensive. Was someone or something in the castle listening, waiting for them? He kept these thoughts to himself.

Graham proceeded to make himself at home, peering in the pantry and in the fridge. "I'm hungry," he said. He came up with a canister labeled OATMEAL COOKIES from the pantry and a large slab of cheddar cheese from the fridge. "We won't take a lot," he said. "Hopefully Mrs. R. won't notice."

They munched on cookies and broke bits off the cheese slab before wrapping it carefully and putting it back. "Okay, where do we start?" Neil said, his mouth full.

"Let's find Aunt Etta's bedroom," Graham said. "I saw a flashlight in the pantry; we'll need it soon." Already the kitchen was growing dim, the brilliant sunlight now blocked by the tall pines as the sun sank in the west.

"I'm glad there's two of us," Graham said, as they started along the hallway that Mrs. Ruff had led them down that morning. Neil felt the same. It was spooky enough when someone was with you.

Their voices echoed in the cavernous gloom – a rude violation of the castle's brooding silence.

At the grand staircase, they stood and gazed up at the landing, where the stairs curved seductively. "Shades of the Roaring Twenties," Graham mused.

"Women in evening gowns and diamond tiaras, pausing there to look down at the men in white tie and tails, waiting for them below."

"With the sound of the orchestra and the clink of champagne glasses in the background," Neil added, having watched more than a few Hollywood movies. "I can see it now." And, for a moment, he even thought he got a whiff of perfume, but the spell passed.

They took the stairs to the second floor and followed a wide carpeted corridor lined with paintings. "Aunt Etta would commandeer one of the better bedrooms, no doubt," Graham said. "This one looks promising."

He opened a double door, which turned out to be a vast walk-in linen closet, its shelves packed with sheets yellowing with age. "Oh, well, even Charlie Chan, ace detective, is sometimes wrong," Graham said, and shut it again.

Farther along, however, they did find a number of large bedrooms – each with its own sitting room, dressing room, and bathroom. In one, Graham, peering in a closet, recognized his aunt's straw hat. "That's hers," he said. "She wears it everywhere. Her favorite summer hat." He looked fixedly at Neil. "Aunt Etta never goes anywhere without that hat."

The closet also held a few dresses and skirts, and

there was a scattering of slips, blouses, and under-clothes neatly folded in the drawers of an antique dresser. A few toiletries remained in the medicine cabinet in the bathroom. There was no sign of a suitcase.

They sat on the four-poster bed and surveyed the room. "Not a lot of her clothes here," Graham said. "So either she really did go away and take most of them with her, forgetting her favorite hat, or . . ."

". . . Or someone else took them to make it look like she'd gone," Neil finished.

"Precisely. In which case, where is she?" Graham said. "And what about her suitcase? All we have are questions."

"There's still the rest of the castle to search," Neil said encouragingly. "Maybe we'll find some answers yet."

"I'm afraid to think about what we might find," Graham said. He gazed up at his aunt's wide-brimmed straw hat, with its colorful silk band, sitting innocently on the top shelf of the closet.

"She never goes anywhere without that hat. . . ."

FOURTEEN

Neil and Graham set out to search the remaining rooms. Eventually, Neil knew, they'd have to face the cellar.

There was nothing more of interest on the second floor, so they headed for the next floor up. Graham switched on the flashlight. He'd been saving the batteries, but now they needed it – the moon peeking in the windows was not enough. The castle had power and it was tempting to turn on some lights, but they couldn't risk attracting attention.

On the third floor, they found a number of smaller guest rooms, the furniture covered with sheets, like the ghosts of the less important visitors who'd been relegated there. They went into every room, looking in cupboards and in shared bathrooms, but all they discovered were spiders in the bathtubs and droppings under the beds from the field mice who'd made cozy nests in the mattresses for the winter.

The main staircase ended at the third floor, but they found back stairs leading up to the fourth floor. "Stairs for the servants, I guess," Neil said, as he followed Graham's circle of light up the steep narrow stairway.

The servants' quarters on the fourth floor were small poky rooms, each with one dormer window. The slanting ceilings forced Graham and Neil to crouch in places. Again, they searched every room. There was only a faded note in one dresser drawer, scribbled in pencil. *Colin, love,* it said. *Come tonight at one o'clock. I'll leave the door unlocked. Betsy.*

"*Uh-huh*, hanky-panky in the servants' quarters," Graham said. "Not nearly as much as in the guests' quarters below, I'll bet."

They finished searching the fourth-floor rooms. Apart from the cellar, the only place left was the attic. At the end of the hall, a rope dangled from the ceiling. Neil pulled on it and a hatch on hinges, with a folding ladder attached, swung down. They looked up apprehensively at the dark opening above.

Graham took a deep breath, climbed the ladder, and stuck his head in. "Hotter than all hell up here," his muffled voice came back. "I can't see a thing. Hand me the flashlight."

Neil passed it up and Graham switched it on. "Yikes!" he shouted, half-falling, half-sliding down the ladder. Something light and translucent drifted down with him.

Neil looked at the object on the floor. It was long and scaly and paper-thin. "Holy smokes! Is that what I think it is?"

Graham nodded. "A snake skin. Gave me quite a start. There's a whole pile of them up there."

"How could snakes get way up there?" Neil wondered aloud.

"Snakes can climb," Graham said. "They probably crawled up between the walls looking for warmth and hibernated there over the winter. Then they shed their skins in the spring and away they went."

"Jeez, maybe there's live ones still up there."

Graham started back up the ladder. "Not likely at this time of year."

Neil followed him reluctantly. There was just room to stand. Cobwebs brushed their faces and dried snake skins crunched underfoot. Graham swung the light around the acres of attic. It picked out old steamer trunks with worn leather straps and boxes overflowing with books. Then, in a far corner, something big and black. In the weak beam of light, it looked like a figure without a head.

They scrambled for the ladder.

Neil stopped abruptly. "Wait a minute," he said, as recognition sunk in. "I know what that is. My mother has one in our attic. It's a dressmaker's dummy."

Graham climbed back up the ladder. "Of course. Difficult to tell what it was in the dark. . . ."

"Of course," Neil said.

Roaming the attic, they came across a rocking horse, its mane and tail moth-eaten, and boxes of expensive-looking toys, barely used. Armies of colorful lead soldiers – British Grenadier Guards, with their tall fur hats, and mounted U.S. Cavalry – were carefully lined up in formation, facing German soldiers with their First World War spiked helmets. Except for the layer of dust on the soldiers' hats, someone could have just finished playing with them.

Neil remembered hearing the story of the young son of the second owner, who vanished mysteriously from the castle years ago. "I'll bet these belonged to the boy who disappeared," he said. He could imagine the boy spending hours in the attic, refighting the Great War with his soldiers. They looked like they were patiently waiting for him to come back and give the order to attack.

In another corner, they found a small suitcase – a smart beige traveling case. Its shiny newness contrasted sharply with the other dusty things in the attic. Graham dropped to his knees and clicked open the latches. The suitcase was jammed with clothes – slips, blouses, skirts, stockings – that appeared to have been stuffed in haphazardly.

"Your aunt's?" Neil asked.

"I suspect so." Graham stared at the case.

"What do you make of its being up here?"

"My guess is that someone hid it here because they wanted Mrs. Ruff to think she'd left on her trip."

They were silent, thinking what this implied.

"Maybe she had two and didn't need this one," Neil said, trying to offer a hopeful suggestion.

Graham gave him a withering look. "So she stuffed this one full of clothes and hid it in one of the farthest corners of the attic?" He stood up. "Well, there's only one more place left to search."

"I know," Neil said. "The cellar." Probably a cold, clammy, creepy place, with dripping water, monster spiders, and scuttling centipedes. He wasn't looking forward to it.

FIFTEEN

Confident they would easily find the stairs leading down to the cellar, Neil and Graham scoured the ground floor, opening every door, peering into every alcove. "There's got to be cellar stairs somewhere," Neil said, as he stood in the hall scratching his head. "Who ever heard of a castle without a cellar?"

Graham agreed. "A dark clammy spooky place usually, like in an Abbott and Costello movie. Maybe the entrance is outside."

So they skirted the outside of the castle, shining the flashlight on the foundation all the way around, without finding any sign of an entranceway. "Baffles me," Graham said. "I can't help feeling we're missing something. . . ."

Back in the kitchen, he sighed. "We've done all we can for now. Might as well get some shut-eye before we have to beat it. I wonder what time Mrs. Ruff and the slave get here in the morning."

Neil yawned. "Dunno, but I'm exhausted."

They went back to the second floor. "Pick a bedroom," Graham said. "There are dozens to choose from. I'll take my aunt's room – maybe it'll give me inspiration while I sleep and I'll wake up with the answer."

They separated, and Neil flopped on the bed in the room next to Graham. Despite his exhaustion, the rattling and grating noises of the old castle kept him awake. What was that creaking sound? Someone coming up the stairs? Were those footsteps outside his door? He had to keep reminding himself that Graham was in the next room, just a step away. Sleeping soundly, no doubt.

Neil didn't fall asleep until the sky began to lighten in the east. Then he slept so soundly that he didn't stir until he heard an abrasive voice calling loudly, "Leonard, where are you?" It was Mrs. Ruff.

Neil leaped out of bed.

A shaft of sunlight was streaming in the bedroom window. *What a time to sleep in!* He tiptoed into

Graham's room. His friend was spread-eagled on his aunt's bed, dead to the world. "Graham," he whispered. "Wake up. They're here!"

Graham's eyes opened slowly. *"Huh*? Who?"

"Shh. It's the Ruffs. Keep your voice down."

Graham sat up. "Holy cow! It's morning already?"

"Yeah. We both slept in."

They crept to the head of the main staircase and listened. From below a swishing sound drifted up, then Mrs. Ruff came into view, wielding a mop. She was pushing a bucket along with her foot as she moved down the hall. They ducked back out of sight. When a floorboard creaked under them, the swishing sound below paused momentarily, then resumed.

"The servants' stairs," Graham mouthed, and Neil nodded. With Mrs. Ruff busy mopping the hall, the kitchen would be empty. They peered cautiously over the banister. She was now mopping the front hall, her back to them. They scooted past the top of the main staircase, where they were in full view from below, and sped along the hall to the back stairs.

At the bottom, Neil eased open the door to the kitchen. *Empty!* He nodded to Graham, and they made a quick dash across the kitchen and out the door. There was still Leonard to watch out for. But the steady *clip, clip* of hedge shears told them where he was. Under the cover of bushes, they got by him.

Once they reached the cove at the back of the island, where Crescent was to pick them up, they breathed easier. "Rather hard on the nerves, this detective business," Graham said. "And we're still no further ahead."

"But you did spot your aunt's favorite hat," Neil reminded him, "*and* her suitcase."

Graham stared out at the placid blue water of the cove, frowning. "Funny though, we never found the cellar. I keep thinking we've missed something."

Neil shrugged. "I don't see how. Maybe there isn't a cellar. Maybe it was too rocky to put one in." He eyed the sky. "The sun's getting up there. Must be ten or so. Where's Crescent, I wonder?"

"I hope she remembers to bring food," Graham said. "I'm starved."

There was nothing to do but wait, keeping an eye out for Leonard. Neil watched the point, around which Crescent would come, willing the bow of *Discovery* to appear. It seemed like hours went by. Finally a boat came around the point, but it wasn't Crescent's.

They heard the *putt, putt, putt* of an engine, then a long narrow double-ended launch, like the ones used by fishing guides, appeared.

In the front, in comfortable wicker chairs one behind the other, sat an older couple. In the center, beside the small inboard engine, a guide steered; behind him sat a teenage boy, and in the stern was a curly-haired girl.

Neil stared. *Crescent!*

SIXTEEN

Crescent waved. The guide shut off the engine, and the launch drifted to a halt in the middle of the cove. The small dinghy it was towing sat rocking in the swell. As Neil and Graham watched, Crescent hauled in the dinghy, climbed into it, and fitted the oars in their slots.

The boy said something to her and she nodded, holding on to the side of the launch while he stepped awkwardly in beside her, rocking the little dinghy so violently that he almost lost his balance. When it settled down, Crescent rowed to shore.

Meantime the older couple in the bow picked up their fishing rods, the guide baited their hooks with minnows from a bucket, and they dropped their lines into the water.

Neil and Graham waited at the water's edge. "Good to see you, Crescent," Neil said, when the dinghy reached shore. "I was getting worried."

"Sorry I'm late, guys," Crescent replied. "I'll explain later. This is Daniel. Daniel, meet my friends, Neil and Graham."

Daniel, who was clutching the gunwales as if his life depended on it, said hi and let go with one hand just long enough to give them a quick wave.

"Climb in," Crescent said.

There was barely room in the little dinghy for the four of them and the gunwales were now mere inches above the water. Daniel looked apprehensive.

"Daniel's from New York," Crescent said, as if that explained everything.

"*New York!*" Graham exclaimed. "Must be neat to see the Empire State Building. A marvel of engineering – they say the top sways only one and a half inches in a 110 mile-an-hour wind."

New York! Neil thought. He'd never met anyone from New York before, the ultimate big city in his mind. It seemed so far removed from Kingsport that it might as well have been on another planet. Not only did it have the world's tallest skyscraper, but also Broadway, Radio City Music Hall and the Rockettes, the Yankees with Joe DiMaggio, and all those movies that open with shots of Manhattan traffic and horn-honking yellow cabs. New York.

Now here was a New Yorker in person. Neil wanted to ask him if there really was a billboard on Broadway that blew smoke rings, but he didn't want to seem like a rube. Who was this guy? he wondered. And why had Crescent come in a launch with him instead of in *Discovery*? Was he after her too?

"The only boats I've ever been in before are those pedal things in Central Park," Daniel said, still clutching the sides tightly. "But they don't rock around like this. My grandparents come up here every year – they're nuts about fishing. Why, I don't know. Sit in a boat all day and dangle a minnow overboard, hoping some fish will come along that's dumb enough to grab it. They're always after me to come with them, so this year I did. I really like them and all, but jeez, fishing!"

Neil could see that Daniel liked talking – a lot more than he liked fishing.

"Hey," Daniel said. "I hear you guys are terrific gumshoes."

Neil wasn't sure whether this was a compliment or an insult.

"You know – detectives, private eyes," Daniel added. "Like in Raymond Chandler's books."

The dinghy pulled up to the launch. They climbed aboard, and Crescent introduced Neil and Graham to Mr. and Mrs. Lonsberg and to Charlie, the guide. Now it was Charlie's boat that was crowded. Neil and Graham sat on the floorboards in the stern with Crescent.

"All set?" Charlie said, poised to start the engine.

"Wait a moment, Charlie!" Mrs. Lonsberg said. "I've got a bite." She jerked on her line and began reeling it in, the rod bending and dipping as the fish fought back gamely. It leaped once, flashing silver and dark green in the sun, then shook the hook loose and was gone. The line hung limp.

"Rats!" Mrs. Lonsberg said. "A nice big bass, too."

"Never mind, dear," her husband said. "Charlie knows where to find lots more."

"We'll just mosey on over to the campground on Lovesick Island," Charlie said. "Then you folks can relax while I fry up some of this fresh catch for lunch." He held up a long string of perch and bass that had been dangling over the side.

They landed at the public dock on the island beside Deadman's. Charlie set up chairs for the Lonsbergs, got a fire going, then began cleaning fish at the water's edge.

"You kids, feel free to explore," Mrs. Lonsberg said. "Come back when you smell fish frying."

"Sure, Gran," Daniel said, and off they went.

Neil and Graham were bursting with curiosity. "So what's happening, Crescent?" Neil said, as soon as they were out of earshot.

"Yeah, we expected to see *Discovery* sail around the point," Graham said. "Why are you in Charlie's boat with the Lonsbergs? Are you keen on fishing?"

Or keen on Daniel? Neil wondered.

Crescent sighed. "Poor *Discovery*. She was stolen last night. The police think it was the German prisoners of war."

"German POWs!" Neil exclaimed. "From the fort?"

Crescent nodded. "Two of them. They escaped yesterday. The police think they'll try to cross to the United States. They probably took the sailboat because a motorboat would have been too noisy. I kept thinking of you guys waiting for me and I didn't know what to do. Then the Lonsbergs – they're in the cottage next door – came to my rescue. Came to your rescue, I should say."

"That was magnanimous of them," Graham said. "They must be wondering what we were doing on Deadman's Island."

"They were kind of curious," Daniel said. "I figured maybe you were just horsing around – you know, summer holidays, nothing to do and all that – but then Crescent told us about the castle and your aunt that you're worried about."

He must have caught Graham's look of concern because he held up his hand. "Hey, don't worry," Daniel said. "I won't tell anyone, neither will my grandparents. I think it's nifty what you're doing. Sneaking around a spooky castle at night looking for clues – sure beats fishing for excitement."

"I hope it was worth it," Crescent said. "What did you find out, Graham?"

"Not much, I'm afraid," Graham said. "We scoured the whole place, top to bottom. There's a gazillion rooms."

"He did find his aunt's favorite hat," Neil added, "which is odd because he says she never goes anywhere without it. Yet there's no sign of her. We found what we think is her suitcase too – in the attic."

"I guess you guys searched the underground passage too, *huh*?" Daniel said casually.

Graham's head jerked up.

SEVENTEEN

—

"What underground passage?" Graham said. "We looked all over for a cellar and couldn't even find that."

"Oh, well, maybe Gramps is confused," Daniel said. "I mean, sometimes his memory's not so hot. But he said there was an underground passage from the castle to the river."

"But what would your grandfather know about the castle? He lives in New York."

"Yeah, weird, isn't it? The guy who built the castle way back? Gramps was a friend of his – they went to Princeton together. The guy was loaded – something to do with railways and all. Back then, when they were rich, they were real rich."

Daniel gestured across the water to where the castle loomed. "He had to be real rich to build that. Anyway, Gramps says his friend was always talking about this castle he was building in the Thousand Islands. He showed Gramps the plans one day and told him there'd even be a hidden passageway to the river. Maybe he thought he'd have to escape from the law in a hurry one day. I mean, they didn't called them robber barons for nothing."

"It's an enigma," Graham said, puzzled. "If your grandfather is right, there's an underground passage. But we couldn't find a cellar, so how do you get to this passage? From the river end?"

"Charlie and Mr. Lonsberg were talking about the castle on the way over," Crescent put in. "Charlie said that back during Prohibition, the island was a drop-off point for smuggled whiskey. There was a rumor that the Canadian smugglers had found an underground tunnel that led to the castle from the river. They would take their boat right into a cave at the back of the island and unload the whiskey into this tunnel – the castle was empty then – and the Americans would pick it up there."

"Shades of Al Capone," Daniel said.

"Maybe we could find the cave," Graham said, "and follow the passage from there back to the castle."

Crescent shook her head. "Unfortunately not. Charlie said the water level in the river has risen since then and the entrance to the cave would be underwater now."

"So we have to find the entrance from the castle end," Graham said. He turned to Neil. "You know what this means?"

Neil nodded. "Another night in the castle."

"Neat. Can I come too?" Daniel said.

Graham and Neil looked at each other. "You really want to?" Graham asked, stalling.

"Sure. We can wait here until dark and then row over in Gramps' dinghy."

"That's his dinghy? I thought it was Charlie's."

"No, it's his. But he'll let me use it."

"But are your grandparents okay with us sneaking into the castle?"

"Heck, it belongs to your aunt, doesn't it?"

"One third of it does."

"I'll just tell them I want to stay with you guys at the campsite. Which is the honest truth. Part of it, anyway."

"I'd better go back with your grandparents," Crescent said. "I'm hoping for news about *Discovery*, and I'm just praying those POWs didn't crack her up on the rocks."

Again Neil'd miss going with Crescent. Would he ever get to be alone with her? he wondered.

Beside him, Daniel sniffed the air. "*Umm.* Charlie's fish fry must be ready. And to think I used to throw up at the thought of eating fish. Let's go. That fresh bass is so good, I'll be having it for breakfast next thing you know."

After the others had left, Neil, Graham, and Daniel kept out of sight on Lovesick Island until they saw the Ruffs' boat go by – Mrs. Ruff erect in the bow like a figurehead, Leonard hunched over the motor.

When the Ruffs' boat disappeared in the direction of the shore, they climbed into the dinghy. Neil manned the oars, Daniel clutched the sides, and Graham, in the bow, watched for the submerged boulder that Charlie, the guide, had warned them about. He didn't see it until it was too late, but as it turned out, the dinghy had such a shallow draft that they didn't even scrape the top of the boulder.

They rowed around Deadman's Island to the cove at the back, where they landed and pulled the dinghy up on the shore, covering it with branches for camouflage. Then they set out for the empty castle.

EIGHTEEN

The three boys scrambled through the bushes to the castle. "So where do we look for this hidden passage?" Graham said.

"Somewhere at the back, I'd guess," Daniel said. "So the owner could beat it while the FBI is coming in the front."

"We should look around outside while it's still light," Neil suggested.

"But what do we look for?" Graham said. "A trapdoor of some sort, I suppose."

"Or a sign saying HIDDEN PASSAGE, ENTER HERE?"

Daniel said, with a grin. "Or WATCH FOR FALLING SKELETONS. *Uh-oh*, sorry, Graham. Dumb thing to say. I forgot it's your aunt we're looking for."

Graham shrugged. "That's okay. I don't really know what I expect to find. Just *something*. Right now, it's all a muddle."

They split up the territory and began to scour the grounds foot by foot, searching for an entrance. The manicured grassy areas were easy. But then they had to go farther out in the scrub, under the towering pines.

"You guys look like you've been wrestling with wildcats," Graham said later, when he and Neil and Daniel had gathered back at the castle. They were scratched, bitten, and sweating, their clothes torn and decorated with burrs.

"I never saw so many thistles," Neil said. "Prickly raspberry bushes too."

"What are those little plants with the shiny leaves?" Daniel asked. "There's this huge patch of them where I was."

"The leaves weren't ternate, were they, Daniel?" Graham said.

"No, they were green."

"I mean, how many on a stem?"

"*Uh* . . . three, I think."

"*Uh-oh*, sounds like you were in a patch of poison ivy. You should wash up. You don't want to break out in a rash tomorrow."

Daniel looked startled. "Jeez, we don't have stuff like that in Central Park."

They stood pondering their next move and swatting at the hordes of mosquitoes that had descended on them as the sun began to set. "I guess the only thing to do now," Neil said, "is search the castle one more time." He set to work again on the lock, and soon they were back in Mrs. Ruff's kitchen.

Graham went straight to the fridge, "Hey, she's made an apple pie. Sure looks good. Do we dare?"

"Maybe she'll blame it on the escaped POWs," Daniel said. "Let's take a chance. Apple pie is good for poison ivy, isn't it?" He was at the sink, diligently washing his arms and legs as Graham had suggested.

They helped themselves to pie. Then, refreshed, they tackled the ground floor once more, looking for a hidden entrance.

"It could be anywhere," Graham said. "Behind a bookcase . . . under a rug . . ."

"Or a button behind a painting that opens a door in the wall," Neil said. "That's a favorite in the movies."

"Or a tile you step on and the floor opens up under you," Daniel added.

They searched the kitchen, the dining room, the billiard room, the study, and the library, looking behind furniture and pictures and under rugs, but they came up empty-handed.

Daniel peered into the room next to the library. "Hey, look at all this stuff!" he said. Scattered about were bumper cars, a colorful tunnel-of-love boat, two merry-go-round horses – one white and placid-looking, the other black and prancing – the car from a roller coaster, even a steam calliope. Bright posters featuring lion tamers, clowns, elephants, and trapeze artists decorated the walls. "Gramps mentioned that his friend collected old circus what-d'you-call-'ems," Daniel said.

"Memorabilia," Graham supplied.

"Yeah, let's have a gander. Great place to hide a secret entrance."

"We looked in there last night," Neil said. "It won't hurt to look again though."

Inside, they began searching. Neil, down on his knees, peered under the bumper cars; Graham pushed the buttons of the calliope; Daniel checked the hooves of the prancing black horse. "Groovy stuff to collect," he said, moving over to the white horse and pulling its tail absentmindedly.

Suddenly, there was a whirring and clanking sound, like gears meshing. The white horse began to tilt sideways, and the rectangular section of floor it was attached to began to swing slowly upwards.

Daniel jumped back out of the way. Across the room, Neil and Graham gaped. "The trapdoor!" Graham exclaimed.

When the trapdoor was fully open, all three crowded around and stared down, but they weren't looking at the cement stairs that disappeared into the darkness below. Their gaze focused on the skeleton, lying at the top of the stairs. . . .

NINETEEN

—

The empty eye sockets stared back at them.

"Cripes, who is *that*?" said Daniel.

"Good God, Graham, can it be . . . ?" said Neil.

"My aunt? No, thank heavens. Aunt Etta is small, but not that small. This looks like a child. Whoever it is, it's been here for months – more likely years, the state it's in."

Neil shifted uncomfortably. It was hard not to look.

At that moment, the whirring and clanking noise began again. They had to back away as the rectangular section of floor swung slowly down and settled into place with a clunk. The white horse attached to it swung back upright and stood there serenely, as if relieved it had finally shared the awful secret it had guarded all these years.

"Well, I'll be darned," Graham said. "The mechanism must be on a timer. You pull the horse's tail and the trapdoor opens, but just long enough for you to go down the steps before it automatically closes behind you."

"Leaving the FBI, who are chasing you, baffled," Daniel added, "while you calmly follow the passage to the boat that's waiting in the cave."

"Very clever," Graham said. "And that's why your grandfather's friend kept it a secret."

"Which still doesn't tell us who that skeleton is," Daniel said. "Or was."

"Not exactly," Graham said. "But I'm beginning to suspect it's the answer to the mystery of the second owner's son – the one who disappeared from the castle and was never found."

"It does add up," Neil said. "I can just imagine the boy playing with the merry-go-round horses, then one day he happens to pull the tail of the white horse and the trapdoor opens." He looked down at the patch of floor under the white horse, imagining the scene that fatal day. "What kid could resist taking a look? Suddenly the floor closes over him . . . and that's that. Poor little guy."

Graham shook his head sadly. "And his father, of course, didn't know about the trapdoor *or* the hidden passage. The man he'd bought the castle from was dead, and the secret of the trapdoor died with him."

For a moment, all three were silent. "I suppose no one could hear the boy's cries," Graham said. "Must be a foot of concrete under the floorboards. And if he gave up calling for help and followed the passage, he wouldn't get far because of the high water level. The curse of the castle, people said, when the boy disappeared. But it wasn't really that at all."

"Or was it?" Daniel said.

They wondered what to do now. "I suppose we should tell the cops," Neil said. "But how do we explain what we were doing here when we found him?"

"In New York, you'd make an anonymous phone call," Daniel said, "then hang up and beat it. Maybe it's different here. It's up to you guys."

"We have to let the police know," Graham said. "But I'd like to explore the underground passage before they arrive. Who knows what else is down there."

"It's a cinch you won't get near it once the cops get here," Daniel said.

The thought of disturbing the boy's bones bothered Neil. "But there can't be anything to do with your aunt down there. It hasn't been opened in years."

"I know," Graham said. "Still, I have this feeling. . . . I guess I don't want to leave any stone unturned, so to speak."

Neil shrugged. "All right, I'm game to go. But the trapdoor will close behind whoever goes down there, so someone has to stay up here to open it again. We sure don't want what happened to the boy to happen to any of us!"

"You two guys go, if you want," Daniel said. "I'll wait up here for you."

After Daniel pulled the horse's tail a second time to open the trapdoor, Neil and Graham stepped gingerly over the skeleton at the top and descended the stairs. A few minutes later, they heard the timer click and the gears begin to whir as the trapdoor closed over their heads.

"Poor little kid, trapped alone down here in the pitch dark," Neil said. He couldn't stop thinking about the boy. He pictured him beating on the cruel concrete with his small fists, his calls for help turning to tears. "He must have been terrified."

"It's creepy enough down here with a light," Graham said, shining the flashlight around the walls. Water dripped from the stones, and strands of soggy green growth hanging from the ceiling brushed their heads.

They had agreed that Daniel would open the door at regular intervals, in case he couldn't hear their shouts when they were ready to leave. Even so, Neil had to fight down a feeling of panic when the heavy trapdoor above them clunked solidly shut.

Now they were moving along the tunnel, over the rough, slippery stone floor. After some distance, the beam of the flashlight picked out an empty cardboard box. It was slumped against the wall, as if it, too, had given up hope of rescue. Part of the label was still visible: *anada's Best Rye Whi* –

"A remnant of Prohibition days," Graham said.

They pressed on, slipping and slithering as the passageway began to slope steeply downwards. Water appeared on the floor, first as puddles, then enough to soak their running shoes. "We must be getting near the cave entrance," Graham said.

Soon they were splashing through several inches of water, where they kept finding debris. A soggy package of Player's Navy Cut Cigarettes, with the familiar picture of a sailor and a life preserver, the wrapping from a Rowntree's five-cent chocolate bar, a waterlogged boat cushion. "Not much point going any farther," Neil said. "It's just going to keep getting deeper."

"I guess," Graham said. "Crescent heard Charlie say the cave itself is underwater now, so the far end of the tunnel will be underwater too. Let's just see what's around the next bend."

They splashed their way there. Ahead was deeper water, but also a glimmer of greenish light. "The opening to the cave, I bet," Graham said. "Okay, I'm satisfied. We've seen all we can. This flashlight's getting dim, anyway. Batteries are going."

By the time they arrived back at the steps, the flashlight beam had faded away completely, but they didn't need it to know that the trapdoor was still closed. They shouted for Daniel and waited, listening for the whir of the gears that would tell them he was opening the trapdoor.

"I guess he doesn't hear us," Neil said, after a few minutes.

"He'll be opening it soon anyway to check on us," Graham replied confidently. "Every ten minutes or so, we agreed. Nothing to do but wait."

They sat in the dark on the bottom step.

"Wish I had a watch," Neil said, a bit later. "It must be all of ten minutes." He kept looking up the steps, though he couldn't see a thing in the absolute darkness. He couldn't even see Graham, who was sitting right beside him. He only knew Graham was there by his rasping, asthmatic breathing in the damp air.

They shouted again, both together at the top of their lungs: "DANIEL!"

No response.

"He's fallen asleep, I'll bet," Graham said.

Neil felt a twinge of panic surface. He pushed it away and tried not to think about what had happened to the skeleton at the top of the stairs.

TWENTY

Eventually, Neil and Graham had to admit that something had gone terribly wrong.

It was so silent, Neil could hear the cracking of Graham's knee joints as he stood up. He felt an urge to reach out and touch him, but he didn't.

"Maybe there's a problem with the mechanism," Graham said. "I'll see what I can do." He gave a forced laugh. "Funny how I use that expression out of habit, even though it's completely inappropriate here."

"*Huh*, what expression?"

"'I'll *see* what I can do.' Why did I say that when I

can't actually *see* a darn thing? It's an example of habit that leads one to . . ."

He's babbling, Neil thought, realizing his friend wasn't as unperturbed as he let on. The thought didn't help his own feeling of panic, which bubbled to the surface again.

A few minutes later, Graham's voice floated down from the top of the stairs. "The mechanism feels normal, far as I can tell. No bent rods, or anything like that." He shouted several more times for Daniel, but his voice grew hoarse and he gave up.

We're trapped, Neil thought. Just like the boy up there was. Something's happened to Daniel and no one else knows we're here . . . no one even knows where the trapdoor is, or how to operate it. We'll end up skeletons too, lying on the steps. Three skeletons in a row.

Later, he sensed that Graham was beside him again. They sat in silence, wrapped in gloomy thoughts. Neil felt as if something was pressing on his chest, making it hard to breathe. Time seemed to have stopped. "What could possibly have happened to Daniel?" he said. "He was our lifeline."

"Goes to show you," Graham said. "Confucius say, when choosing lifeline, make sure no weak links in same."

"What do you mean 'weak links'?"

"Just that. When you come right down to it, how much do we know about Daniel?"

Neil was startled by the idea. He tried to imagine Daniel deliberately walking away and leaving them there. *Was Graham serious?* "But Daniel wouldn't abandon us," he said. "He's a friend of Crescent's."

"Is he? Or is he someone who just happens to be in the cottage next door and who she's met for the first time – a guy who hates fishing, yet who comes here, supposedly, to be with his grandparents who do nothing but fish all day."

Neil shifted uneasily. Being trapped down here with the boy's skeleton must be working on Graham's mind. It was making him paranoid. "I just can't believe Daniel would abandon us," he said.

"That's because you're naïve. You accept people at face value. An admirable quality, but not when you're a detective investigating a possible crime."

"But –"

"Just consider the possibilities: Mr. Lonsberg's been coming here every summer for years. He meets Jake Grimsby, or maybe Carson Snyder . . . more likely Snyder. Snyder learns that Lonsberg knew the original owner of the castle and likes to talk about it. He cultivates Lonsberg, they become friends, and Snyder learns about the secret passage."

"All right," Neil said. "I suppose that's possible, but it's no reason Daniel would –"

"*Ah*, but there's more. You and I come nosing around –"

"But Snyder doesn't even know we're here."

"He's found out from Mrs. Ruff. She phones him and tells him we're snooping around. Snyder and Grimsby realize we're a danger to their plans. They tell Lonsberg about us, say we're spreading lies about them, and we need to be taught a lesson. They include Daniel in their little scheme, and he agrees to lead us to the secret passage and leave us trapped there – trapped temporarily, he thinks, because Snyder says he'll let us out in the morning, only he has no intention to."

"Sounds awful far-fetched to me, Graham."

"Does it? Who knew that pulling the white horse's tail opened the trapdoor? *Daniel*. And who suggested that he be the one to stay behind to open the trapdoor for us? *Daniel again*. Still skeptical? All right, consider this possibility. Snyder makes a deal with Lonsberg. He and Daniel get rid of us and the Lonsbergs get to stay in the castle every summer for free. Lonsberg's fascinated by the castle, and he can stay in it while he fishes his golden years away –"

"Now hold on," Neil said. "I may be naïve, but you can't tell me that Daniel's the sort of person who would walk away and leave us here. I just don't believe it. And as for your ridiculous story of a plot . . ."

"Have it your way, then," Graham said, and Neil could tell from his voice that he was moving up the stairs, away from him. "I suppose you'll keep making excuses for Daniel until we breathe our last down here."

This isn't like Graham, Neil thought. His mind's gone squirrelly. Small wonder. Trapped in this creepy place, you start imagining all kinds of things. How could he have expected him to remain the same calm, rational Graham? Next thing, he, Neil, will be talking nonsense himself. It was up to him to act while he could still think straight.

"Something's happened to Daniel, and there's only one way we're going to get out of here," he said finally.

Graham's voice came down from the top of the stairs. "What way is that?"

Neil stood up and felt for the walls of the passage-way. "We'll have to follow the tunnel to the end and swim out. Through the cave."

"Swim out? But the cave is underwater now, and the end of the tunnel will be, too. Who knows how far you'd have to swim underwater? How long can you hold your breath, anyway? The thought of it gives me the shivers."

"Well, staying here gives *me* the shivers."

"But by staying here, there's a chance Daniel might change his mind and open the trapdoor," Graham said. His conviction that Daniel had deserted them seemed to be fading, Neil noticed. Maybe he'd been shocked back to reality by the thought of having to swim underwater through the cave.

"There's a chance we can get out by swimming, too," he said.

"True," Graham admitted. "You choose your poison, I guess."

"Yeah, die fast or die slowly." Neil felt better talking about it, getting it out on the table instead of letting it go around and around inside his head. Either way was a gamble – try to swim out underwater, or sit here and wait to see if Daniel shows up.

"I'd go with you," Graham said, "but when it comes right down to it, I couldn't bring myself to plunge in. I'm not as good a swimmer as you. The way I flounder around in the water, I'd never make it."

"I can understand that. I'll go it alone," Neil said. "See you later, then."

"Wait! If you've really made up your mind to risk it," Graham said, "I'll keep you company as far as the end of the tunnel. It's the least I can do."

"No, Graham, you'd better stay here, in case the trapdoor does open. Holler if it does – I may still be there, standing in water up to my crotch, trying to get up my nerve."

Graham came down the stairs. "God, Neil, are you sure?"

"I can do it," Neil said. They both understood he wouldn't know that until either he surfaced outside, or ran out of air and found it was too late to turn back. "And the next thing you know," he went on, "I'll be up there opening the trapdoor for you . . . I hope," he muttered under his breath.

Neil started to feel his way along the passage.

TWENTY-ONE

As he'd imagined, Neil was standing up to his crotch in water, shivering, trying to get up his nerve. It reminded him of swimming expeditions on the 24th of May holiday, when it would take him forever to plunge into the icy water of Lake Ontario in that yearly ritual.

But icy water wasn't holding him back here. It was fear of the unknown. How far would he have to swim underwater? How long before he could surface and breathe again?

After he'd left Graham, Neil made his way along the tunnel until there was water underfoot. By then, the total blackness of the upper tunnel had lightened slightly, enough for him to dimly make out the moss-covered stones of the walls.

From there the passage sloped steeply downwards, and the water deepened rapidly. He had already stripped off his shoes and pants, leaving them behind. The less hindrance, the better. When the water reached the top of his legs, Neil stopped and stared ahead. It was like looking through a solid block of thick, dark green glass, which transmitted a hint of light from somewhere distant. How far was it to the source of that light – the mouth of the cave and the outside?

"Come on, Neil," he said, "do it." He plunged in and started to swim. The airspace between him and the top of the passage shrank rapidly. Two feet of air, then one foot, then his head bumped the stones over-head. It was now or never.

He filled his lungs, duck-dived, then swam under-water as fast as he could, breast-stroking with his arms, frog-kicking with his legs. He could sense the top of the tunnel just above him and knew there was no airspace there at all now.

He swam on, the pressure to breathe out mount-ing. Eyes fixed on the way ahead, he prayed for an opening, a change in the light – anything to indicate the end. His ears rang; he felt faint. Should he turn back before it was too late?

A cloud of bubbles burst from his mouth. Immediately, a terrible urge to breathe in again took over, and he fought against it. He stroked and frog-kicked desperately, knowing the decision had been made for him now. He'd never make it back. He could only go forward. Was this the end? *Air. Air. Air. Where is it? Please, God, air.*

Then suddenly, just ahead, a patch of lighter water – or was he hallucinating? Three more strokes and he was there. *An opening!* The end of the passage. He swam through it into the cave and shot upwards. Up and up he went.

Neil broke the surface, his head cracking sharply against the top of the cave. *An airspace!* Not much of an airspace, but enough. Gasping, half-choking, he filled his lungs. Precious, life-giving air.

He stayed there, treading water, his head thrust back gulping breath after breath. How wonderful it was to breathe again. He'd made it! Now he felt as if he could do anything – find his way out of the cave, free Graham from his prison, and, best of all, be with Crescent again. The way he felt now, he could conquer the world.

When his heartbeat had slowed from its frantic pace, he dove again and kept swimming toward the light. On and on until he ran out of breath a second time. He had to find the air pocket at the top of the cave again, and quickly. He headed up, but as he did, something brushed against his face. He pushed it away. Then he saw what it was – a woman's shoe. Beside it was another one. Neil grabbed for it, but it drifted out of reach. His lungs were bursting. He shot on up.

Up and up he went. Above him, the dark water lightened gradually. Then he broke the surface, carefully this time, the top of his head still tender.

But there was no stone ceiling to bang his head against this time. A wave slapped him in the face. Above him, the night sky sparkled with stars, and a nearly full moon hovered in the western sky. It was the loveliest sight he'd ever seen.

He was out.

TWENTY-TWO

Neil saw that he'd emerged by the cliffs at the back of the island. To his left, the cliffs tapered down to the shore of the cove, where he and Graham and Daniel had landed earlier. Was it just last night? It seemed a lifetime ago.

He swam parallel to the shore until he reached the cove. Climbing out, he stood on the smooth slab of granite, ignoring the chilly, predawn breeze, and relished being alive. I'll always remember this moment, he thought, feeling as if he'd emerged from the water a brand-new person – like the snakes in the attic that had sloughed off their old skin.

He would have liked to rest, but there wasn't time – he had to free Graham and find out what had happened to Daniel. He set out in the dark, barely noticing the rocks and roots that bruised his bare feet.

When Neil stepped inside the back door of the castle, the same eerie silence as before greeted him. Again he had the impression that someone or something was there. The feeling was even stronger this time, and he had to remind himself that they had searched all through the castle the night before and found nothing. Nothing alive, that is . . .

Still the feeling persisted. He took a few steps and peered into the gloom of the kitchen. Suddenly there was a noise, like that of a chair scraping across the floor. His skin prickled, but he stood his ground. "Daniel?"

Again the scraping sound. It was followed by a muffled voice. *"Oom haar."*

"Is that you, Daniel?" Now he could see a dark shape, short and bulky, making jerky movements. As he edged closer, the shape became a figure on a chair. Then the figure became Daniel himself, bound to the chair and gagged.

"Daniel! It *is* you."

"Tak oof ta gaaa," Daniel said.

"Hang on, I'll find a knife and cut you loose," Neil said.

Daniel waggled his head vigorously. *"Oonta ta gaaa firr."*

"Untie the gag first? Oh, sure." Neil felt for the knot behind Daniel's head. He worked at it until it gave way and the gag, a dishcloth, fell off.

"Man, that thing hurt!" Daniel said. "Now the ropes."

Yanking open drawers until he found a sharp knife, Neil cut the ropes. Daniel stretched. "What a relief," he said, rubbing his wrists. "I was worried sick about you guys down there. How did you get out, anyway?" He took in Neil's wet underpants and T-shirt. "You swam?"

"It was the only way out," Neil said. "But Graham's still there."

Daniel leaped up, staggered, and almost fell, his joints stiff from being bound to the chair. "Poor Graham must be going batty. We gotta get him out of there." Walking stiff-legged, like Frankenstein, he hurried, as best he could, out of the kitchen, muttering, "Down there all alone, dark and all, thinking he'll die there and cursing me."

Neil hurried after him. "But what happened to you, Daniel? Who tied you up? And where are they now?" He looked around apprehensively.

"Tell you later" was all Daniel would say, "after we get Graham out." He went straight to the white horse and yanked its tail. He and Neil waited, staring at the rectangle of floor where the trapdoor would open.

Nothing happened.

Daniel gave the tail another tug. Still nothing – no whirring motor, no clanking gears, no rising trapdoor.

"*Uh-oh*," Daniel said.

The mechanism's kaput, Neil thought. The trapdoor won't open. His mind raced ahead. He'd have to swim back in and get Graham out that way, somehow. Could he face all that again?

"What a royal pain in the ass," Daniel groaned, giving the tail several more impatient tugs. "Crumby thing's quit on us. What d'you suppose has gone wrong with it?"

"What a time for this to happen," Neil said in dismay.

"We might have to borrow one of those drills they use to dig up streets," Daniel said.

Neil tried to remember what he'd learned about electrical circuits in manual-training class. Even if he did figure out how to get at the wiring, it was too dark in there to tell one wire from another. "We need a flashlight," he said. "But it's down there with Graham – and the batteries are dead."

"Let's take a chance and turn on the lights in here," Daniel said. He went to the door and felt around on the wall for the switch. "Okay?"

"Sure, do it," Neil said. So what if the lights were seen from the shore. He heard the click of the switch and closed his eyes against the expected burst of light. But when he opened them again, the room was still dark.

A light did dawn in his brain, however. "The power's off!" he exclaimed. "No wonder the trapdoor wouldn't open."

"I'll bet those guys did it."

"What guys?"

"The guys who tied me up. I heard them fiddling with the fuse box in the kitchen before they left."

"Then all we have to do is turn the power back on and we're in business. Where's this fuse box?"

"C'mon, I'll show you."

They hurried to the kitchen and Daniel pointed out the fuse box in the corner of the pantry. Neil opened it and peered at the circuits. His face fell. "They took the fuses out! Every one of them."

"What? Those jerks! They made sure I'd stay in the dark even if I did get free. Guess they didn't want me signaling for help with the lights."

"There's not a fuse left," Neil said, in disgust. Then his foot kicked something and sent it flying across the pantry, where it dinged against a canister of flour. He felt around on the floor. "Hey, they dropped one!" he said triumphantly, holding up the fuse. "You go in the circus room and shout when the lights go on."

He tried the fuse in each of the circuits in the fuse box until a shout from Danny told him he'd found the right one.

By the time Neil got there, the white horse was tilting and the trapdoor rising.

TWENTY-THREE

Even before the trapdoor was fully open, Graham's head appeared. His eyes were squinched against the light, like a mole who'd just come up from a long spell underground.

"Is that you finally, Daniel? Where've you been?" Graham said, although it was actually the white horse's rear end he was addressing. "Can't see a thing. Turn off the lights, will you, before they blind me. Any sign of Neil? I'm worried about him. He's trying to swim out – a mad but courageous idea."

"I'm here," Neil said. "Hang on, I'll turn the lights off."

"Neil! You made it! Good going. I was really worried. . . . *Ah*, that's better," Graham said, as the lights went off. "Thank God you're out, Neil. Rather glad to be out myself, as a matter of fact. I was beginning to think I'd perish down there. Like this poor little fellow here." He carefully stepped over the skeleton and emerged. "I brought your clothes up, hoping you'd be here," he said, handing Neil his pants and shoes. "But what happened to you, Daniel?"

"I was tied up," Daniel said.

"Tied up?" Graham looked puzzled.

"And the first thing he did after I untied him," Neil said, "was rush in here to open the trapdoor for you. Only it wouldn't open. They'd taken out the fuses and –"

"Who'd taken out the fuses?" Graham said.

"The guys who tied me up, of course" Daniel said. "But what about your aunt? Did you find any trace of her?"

Graham shook his head. "No, nothing. But these guys who tied you up – who were they?" He jumped as the automatic timer kicked in and the trapdoor began to shut. "This room gives me the creeps, all of a sudden," he said. "Let's adjourn to the kitchen and you can tell me what happened. Then we have to decide what to do about the skeleton."

As the trapdoor descended, Neil looked down at the skeleton in sympathy. He hated to see it shut in again. "Don't worry," he said. "We'll be back. And I'll see that you're taken out of there and sent back to your family, where you belong. That's a promise."

Graham and Daniel looked at him strangely.

Neil had no idea how he would find the boy's family now, but he would do it somehow, he told himself. He had to, so that the boy's spirit would know he hadn't been forsaken. Maybe it was just the draft from the trapdoor closing, but it seemed to him that the skull nodded, as if it understood.

They sat around the kitchen table in the dark, the three of them, while Daniel related his story.

"After you guys went down into the tunnel," he said, "I stayed in the room so I could open the trapdoor every ten minutes or so, like we agreed. Then I heard a noise in the kitchen, so I went down the hall to see if an animal had gotten in, or what. Next thing I knew, someone grabbed me from behind and pinned my arms. At first I thought it was the cops and they'd found out about us breaking in. Then I heard these two guys talking in a foreign language, which I finally figured out was German."

"German!" Graham said. "They must have been the POWs that escaped from the fort."

"The same ones that took Crescent's boat, probably," Neil said. "But why did they come here? And where are they now?"

"Gone," Daniel said. "They came looking for food, I think. But they must have heard me coming and grabbed me. They tied me up with some clothesline and used an old dishcloth as a gag. *Yuck!* I can still taste it." He reached for one of Mrs. Ruff's cookies to get rid of the taste.

"One of them spoke a little English. He wasn't a bad guy. He said they were sorry to do this to me, but they needed time to get away. They raided the fridge and wolfed down some stuff, and I heard them fiddling with the fuse box in the pantry. Then they went out the back door, and that was the last I saw of them."

"They're probably over the border by now, heading for a big city where they can blend in," Graham said.

"I tried to wiggle free, but they'd tied me up good," Daniel said. "I couldn't do anything but sit there thinking what a fix we were in – you guys stuck underground, me stuck here, where that Ruff person would find me in the morning and call the cops, and we'd all end up in the clink. Then I heard someone coming in the back and I thought *what now?* What a relief when Neil waltzes in in his underwear!"

"None too soon, either," Graham said. "I was going nuts down there, with only the skeleton for company. I even started talking to it. Funny what the mind does when you're stranded in the pitch dark for half the night. I was convinced Neil was lying on the bottom of the cave, drowned." He gave Neil an admiring glance. "That must have been an awful scary underwater swim."

Neil shrugged. "It was a bit rough." He told them about making it through the tunnel into the cave and from there to the outside. Then he remembered the woman's shoes he'd seen in the water.

Graham was startled. "What? That could be important!"

"I know. I would have gone after them, but I had to find air in a hurry."

"What did they look like?"

"A woman's shoes. They looked new."

"High heels, saddle shoes, straps, laces, or what?"

Neil thought for a moment, trying to picture the drifting shoes. "They were what my mother would call good sensible shoes. You know, low heels, leather – slip-ons, I think. They couldn't have been in the water that long – they looked in good shape."

"I hate to say it," Daniel said, "but those shoes could be a big fat clue, Graham."

Graham looked pale. "I don't like to think what they could mean."

They sat in silence, contemplating all that had happened that night.

"So what do we do now?" Neil said, after a while. "About the skeleton, I mean."

Graham made a face. "Not much choice. We've got to report it. So I guess we wait for dear Mrs. Ruff to show up and get her to call the cops."

"I can just imagine what she'll say when she finds us here," Neil said.

"I can't wait to meet her," Daniel said. "She sounds charming."

"And she's got a particular hate on for me," Graham said. "The only one she likes is Crescent. Too bad she's not here."

"Maybe she'll show up in the morning," Neil said, brightening at the thought.

"She'll probably come in Charlie's launch with Gran and Gramps," Daniel said. "I hope so, anyway. She's a looker, that Crescent."

Neil felt the old jealousy coming back.

They waited on the dock, watching the sun come up. It wasn't long before the distant whine of an outboard shattered the dawn quiet. It grew in volume and then the Ruffs' boat rounded the point, with Mrs. Ruff in the bow, arms crossed. As soon as she caught sight of them, she turned and said something to Leonard. He put the motor in idle and let the boat drift, fifty feet from the dock.

Mrs. Ruff's angry voice ricocheted across the water.

"Miss Stone's not here, and I told you kids yesterday that this is private property," she shouted.

"This is an emergency," Graham called back.

Mrs. Ruff ignored him. "You had your warning. I'm going to call the police right now. You're trespassing." She turned to her husband. "Head back to shore, Leonard."

"Good," Graham called. "You do that, Mrs. Ruff. And while you're at it, you'd better let them know we found a skeleton in the castle."

Leonard didn't need any more instructions when he heard that. He headed straight for the dock.

"Is this some kind of joke?" Mrs. Ruff said, as the bow nudged the side.

"I wish it was," Graham said. "But it's the truth."

"I don't believe you," she said, heaving her bulk onto the dock. "You're just trying to get out of the trouble you're in. Show me this skeleton."

"No, you go back and call the police first," Graham insisted. They stood eyeball to eyeball. "If you don't, the responsibility is on your shoulders."

Reluctantly, Mrs. Ruff got back in the boat. "I'll call the police all right. But if you're making this up, you'll be –" Her threat was drowned out by the motor as Leonard opened up the throttle and the craft roared away.

TWENTY-FOUR

Sergeant Simpson, one-half of the Riverview Police Force – the larger half – eyed Daniel suspiciously. "No kidding, officer, I just happened to tug the tail of this white horse," Daniel was saying. "And the next thing I knew, a trapdoor opened." He reached for the tail. "Here, I'll show you."

"Wait!" the sergeant barked. "You'll do it when I tell you to, not before." Neil, watching from the doorway, thought *he still doesn't believe us*.

Sergeant Simpson had been like that from the moment he stepped out of the Ruffs' boat and confronted the three boys on the dock – his attitude influenced, no doubt, by Mrs. Ruff's tale of her run-in with Graham the day before. Not helping was the fact that here were three teenage boys and, in the sergeant's opinion, teenage boys were behind practically all of his problems in the town of Riverview.

Walking up to the castle, the sergeant had fired a stream of questions at them. "You'd been warned by Mrs. Ruff that this was private property, so what are you doing here?"

"Looking for my aunt," Graham said. "I told Mrs. Ruff that yesterday."

"But she told you your aunt wasn't here. How did you get in the castle?"

"By the back door," Graham said, boldly.

"Mrs. Ruff swears that all the doors were securely locked when she left," the sergeant said.

The boys looked at each other. "The lock on the back door isn't much good," Neil said. "I just touched it and it flew open."

The sergeant stopped. "You broke in! That's a serious charge."

Mrs. Ruff smirked.

"My good man," Graham said. Neil cringed – that wasn't exactly the best way to address Sergeant Simpson. He saw the sergeant's look darken, but Graham went blithely on. "We simply *had* to get inside. You see, I have reason to believe something happened to my aunt while she was here. She's disappeared and –"

"Your aunt left," Mrs. Ruff interjected. "I told you that yesterday. There wasn't a soul in the castle when I went home last night. They're making all this up, Sergeant. Miss Stone left on a trip. As for all this talk of a skeleton – why, I've cleaned this castle from top to the bottom, and if there was anything like a skeleton in here, I'd have come across it long ago."

"Well, we'll soon find out," the sergeant said. "You boys show me where this so-called skeleton is. And if it turns out you've brought me here for nothing, there'll be trouble."

They reached the massive front door and Mrs. Ruff flourished a great round key ring jammed with keys. "Don't bother with those; the door's open," Graham said. "We came out that way." She glared at him, but pushed the door open.

Inside, the boys led the sergeant along the hall to the room with the merry-go-round horses. Daniel explained about the trapdoor and reached for the white horse's tail to demonstrate.

"Wait," said the sergeant, as he approached the horse and examined the tail suspiciously. "You're trying to tell me that all you did was pull this tail?"

Mrs. Ruff snorted. "A likely story."

"Yes, sir," Daniel said. "I yanked it like this." Again he took hold of the tail.

"I said wait!" the sergeant barked. He was beginning to worry that there might be something to the boys' story after all. It was the last thing he wanted. All he'd expected to have to do was puncture holes in their story, then take them in and give them a good scare about trespassing.

Stalling for time, the sergeant turned to Graham and Neil. "And just where were you two during this tail-pulling business?"

"Over there," Graham said, pointing. "I was examining the calliope, and Neil was looking under the bumper cars."

"Then go there now. I want everything exactly as it was." The sergeant turned back to Daniel. "All right. Now go ahead."

"Sir," Graham called from across the room. "You'd better move out of the way."

"When I want to hear from you, I'll tell you," the sergeant ordered. He nodded at Daniel.

Daniel pulled. The sergeant leaned against the horse, waiting. For a moment nothing happened, except a muffled clanking sound. "Just as I thought – *whoa!*" the sergeant yelled. For the horse had suddenly began to tilt. He threw his arms around its neck for support as the floor under him began to swing upwards.

A few moments later, the trapdoor was upright and the horse was horizontal, with the sergeant sprawled on top of it.

His face purple, he struggled to his feet and glowered at Daniel. But before he could say anything, there was a loud scream. Mrs. Ruff was pointing, wide-eyed.

The sergeant looked. His mouth fell open. "What is that!"

"The skeleton," Daniel said, calmly.

"But who is it, and what's it doing there?"

Graham came over. "If I had to guess," he said, "I'd say it's very likely the missing son of the second owner – you know, the young boy who disappeared from the castle years ago and was never seen again."

"*Humph*," the sergeant grunted. "I remember that case. It was ruled at the inquest that the boy must have fallen in the river and drowned." He eyed them suspiciously. "His body never surfaced. It wouldn't surprise me if you boys found it somewhere else and put it there on purpose."

"Why would we do that?" Neil asked innocently.

"Why do boys do anything?" the sergeant muttered. He bent to examine the skeleton. When he straightened up, he pointed down the stairs. "What else is down there?"

"A tunnel," Graham said. "It goes to the river."

"How do you know?"

"We followed it, Neil and I. And then Neil –"

"And what did you find?" the sergeant interrupted. The extra work he'd be saddled with because of this unwelcome discovery was just beginning to sink in.

"All we found was an empty whiskey carton," Graham said. "Then we came back and waited for Daniel to open the trapdoor for us. It closes automatically on a timer, as you'll see in a minute. By the way, you'd better move, Sergeant. . . ."

Just then, the gears started clanking and the trapdoor began closing. This time, the sergeant moved away smartly.

Graham continued his story. "Daniel stayed up here to open the trapdoor for us, but it didn't happen. Daniel had been tied up by the POWs, but we didn't know that, so Neil decided –"

The sergeant started. "Did you say POWs? They were here? Why didn't you tell me? Every policeman for miles around has been looking for those guys. Where are they now?"

"Far away, I assume," Graham said placidly. "Probably in the sailboat they stole."

"But what were they doing here?"

"Looking for food, I guess," Daniel said. "They must have seen there were no boats in the boathouse and thought the castle was empty. They grabbed me when I went to see what the noise was in the kitchen and tied me up. Then they got some stuff out of the fridge and left."

Sergeant Simpson turned to Mrs. Ruff. "This changes everything. Leonard will have to take me back to shore immediately. I'll need to use your phone to report the POW sighting. Then I'll get hold of the coroner to come and look at this skeleton."

"There's the missing person to search for too," Graham said.

The sergeant's eyes bulged. "The what?"

"My aunt is missing and I fear that –"

"I told you," Mrs. Ruff broke in, "your aunt left here last Sunday."

"I wish you were right," Graham said. "But if she left, why is her suitcase hidden in the attic and her favorite hat still in her closet?"

Mrs. Ruff was clearly surprised to hear about the suitcase and the hat, but that didn't stop her. "I don't know about that," she shot back. "But I know her boat and her car are gone."

"That may be," Graham said, "but Neil saw what might well turn out to be her shoes in the river. I'm afraid my aunt has met with foul play and you, Sergeant, must get a police diver over here right away."

"Look here, son, *I'll* decide what I must do," the sergeant huffed. It was apparent from his glowering expression that this was all a bit much for him – a skeleton, escaped POWs, a missing person, and now this smart-aleck kid telling him what to do. "And I've no intention of taking officers off the search for the POWs to look for a supposed missing person just because you saw some shoes in the river. They could be anybody's. So keep your noses out of police business in future, or I'll charge you with . . ."

The sergeant paused, trying to recollect what exactly he could charge them with. "Obstructing justice," he finally came up with. "Plus breaking and entering . . . and mischief."

"But my aunt –" Graham began.

"You've got your aunt on the brain, young man," Mrs. Ruff said. "Get it through your thick skull that she's not here and stop playing detective. Leave that to the police."

"Right," Sergeant Simpson said. "Now, Ruby, about this skeleton. I'm going to have to get in touch with the present owners of the castle and have them come here for questioning. If you'd just give me their addresses and phone numbers . . ." He whipped out a battered notebook.

"Well," Ruby Ruff said, "as for Miss Stone, she didn't leave a forwarding address. But the other two live in

Kingsport. Their phone numbers are in the kitchen. I'll just get them for you."

"I'll come with you," the sergeant said, sensing a chance for a reviving cup of coffee and a slice of Ruby's famous apple pie. "Then I'll get Leonard to take me back to shore."

Mrs. Ruff paused at the door to the hall and pointed to the three boys. "What about them? You going to take them with you and charge them with trespassing?"

"Not right now, Ruby, I've got too many other things to do," the harried sergeant said. "Keep them here for now."

"You expect *me* to keep them here?" Mrs. Ruff screeched.

"But we're hungry, Sarge," Daniel protested. "We haven't even had breakfast. Couldn't we just row over to our campsite for something to eat?"

"You can eat here," the sergeant said in exasperation. "Give them something to keep them quiet, Ruby."

"You want me to *feed* them too?" Mrs. Ruff howled.

The sergeant, seeing his chances for a cup of coffee and a piece of Ruby's pie disappearing fast, wrote down the phone numbers for Grimsby and Snyder and left. "I'll be back with the coroner," he said over his shoulder. "Just don't let those boys off the island."

TWENTY-FIVE

"Where do you think you're going?" Mrs. Ruff said. The boys had just finished demolishing the rest of her apple pie, which she had reluctantly served them, and were heading out the back door. "You heard what Sergeant Simpson said. You're not to leave the island."

"We're only going down to the shore," Neil said. "Don't worry, we won't leave."

"Why would we?" Graham added. "We like it here."

"You bet. Great apple pie," Daniel said. "Thanks."

Mrs. Ruff grunted.

They made their way through the bushes to the cove, where they'd landed the night before. "Will your grandparents find us here, Daniel?" Neil said.

"They'll expect us to be on Lovesick Island at the campsite," Daniel said. "But they usually go by here on the way, and we can flag them down. Be hours yet though. Gran and Gramps don't move that fast in the morning."

The sun was halfway to the zenith, the powder blue sky cloudless. It promised to be another bright sunny day. The boys settled down to wait. Neil yawned. "It was a long night." He and Daniel both lay back on the warm smooth rock and closed their eyes.

But Graham paced restlessly. "I can't stop thinking about the shoes you bumped into, Neil. What did you say they looked like?"

"Just women's shoes, low heels, loafers," Neil said groggily. He tried to picture the shoes, which had been suspended like fruit in a bowl of jello. "They looked new, but like I said, all I cared about then was finding air before I passed out. I wish now I'd grabbed one of them."

"It's not likely the obtuse Sergeant Simpson will do anything about it," Graham groused. "But someone should dive down there and find them. I hate to say it, but they could be Aunt Etta's, which would mean . . ." He couldn't bring himself to say the fateful words.

Graham stopped pacing and looked down at Neil. "I'd go, but I'm hopeless at swimming underwater."

Neil remembered how close he'd come to not making it out of the cave the first time. The thought of going back there was not pleasant.

"Maybe we could get the cops to fire a cannon," Daniel interjected. "Just in case there is a body down there."

They both turned to look at Daniel, sprawled on the rock. "What!?"

"Fire a cannon," Daniel repeated. "Haven't you guys read *The Adventures of Huckleberry Finn*? When Huck ran away, they thought he'd drowned in the Mississippi, so they fired a cannon to bring his body to the surface. Course it didn't come up because Huck hadn't drowned – he was hiding on an island watching it all."

"The British navy used cannons too, come to think of it," Graham said. "The shock wave was supposed to burst the gallbladder and produce gas, which made the body rise, but that's been pretty well disproven."

"Suppose there really is a body to go with the shoes," Neil said. "How long would it be before it comes to the surface by itself?"

"There's no easy answer," Graham, the fount of information, said. "It depends on a lot of things – the water temperature, whether the person is fat or skinny. . . . Some skinny ones never do surface, especially if the water's cold. But we're getting ahead of ourselves. Enough of this talk about a body. Somehow we have to find those shoes and see what they tell us."

Neil got up reluctantly. "Then I'd better go back and have another look," he said quickly, before he could change his mind.

Graham sat in the little dinghy, peering down into the water. He couldn't see anything, however, as a breeze was rippling the surface. The minutes were ticking by since Neil had disappeared into the depths.

He had made careful note of their position when Neil stopped rowing and said that this was about where he'd surfaced after his underwater swim. Then he'd plunged overboard, leaving Graham to take the oars.

Now, manning the oars awkwardly, Graham struggled to keep the dinghy opposite the same pine tree onshore – the stunted one growing out of the rock face. The little dinghy, however, was rebellious and refused to go where he wanted.

But where was Neil? Why hadn't he come up for air? Graham berated himself for letting him go down there a second time. Why hadn't he kept quiet about it? He might have known that conscientious Neil would feel it his duty to go.

It seemed forever before there was a sudden erup-
tion and a form shot out of the depths, like a dolphin
after a flying fish. Neil swam over, hauled himself
into the dinghy, and collapsed on the floorboards. He
shook his head in answer to Graham's inquiring look.
"No . . . luck," he said, between pants. "Not a sign of
. . . the shoes. . . . I'll have . . . a rest . . . then try again."

"No!" Graham said firmly, rowing away as fast as he
could, the dinghy veering this way and that. "It's too
dangerous, Neil. You gave it a good shot. We'll have to
think of something else." He paused. "Maybe you'd
better take the oars, or we'll never get back. This
darned boat has a mind of its own."

TWENTY-SIX

When they arrived back at the cove, Daniel was perched on the rock, watching for Charlie's launch. Before long, they heard the *putt, putt, putt* of an inboard engine, and the launch appeared around the point.

Daniel jumped to his feet. "There they are! And Crescent's with them." The boys all waved wildly until Charlie spotted them and turned into the cove. As the launch neared the shore, he cut the motor and let her drift. "Too rocky to come any farther," Charlie called to them.

"We'll row out," Daniel called back. He could see his grandparents exchanging puzzled looks, wondering, no doubt, what they were doing on Deadman's Island.

They climbed into the dinghy, and Neil rowed out to the launch. He shipped the oars and came alongside.

"Daniel," Mrs. Lonsberg said sharply, "what on earth are you doing here?"

"We came over to look for Graham's aunt, Gran," Daniel said. "We didn't find her, but a whole lot of other things happened. And guess what, Gramps? We found the secret underground passage!"

"You did?" Gramps exclaimed. "That's exciting! So my memory was right after all." He looked pleased.

But Mrs. Lonsberg wasn't pleased. "You went in the castle, Daniel!" she said. "That's private property. I hope you had permission."

Daniel looked away. "Well, sort of . . ."

"What do you mean, 'sort of'?"

"Well, *uh*, I mean, we didn't have permission when we first went in, but we do now. In fact, Sergeant Simpson told us not to leave the island."

"What! Are you in trouble with the police?"

"Not exactly," Daniel said, at which point Graham spoke up.

"It was all my idea, Mrs. Lonsberg. It's a long story – we found more than we bargained for – but as Daniel said, we're not supposed to leave, so why don't you come ashore and we can explain what happened."

"Let's go, dear," Mr. Lonsberg said.

"If I can tag along, I'd sure like a chance to see the castle!" Charlie said.

So Neil rowed Graham and Daniel back to shore, then made two more trips – the first to ferry the Lonsbergs in and then Crescent and Charlie, who had set out a sturdy anchor in the meantime. "I gotta see this secret passage you boys discovered," Charlie said, on the trip in. "I've always wondered if there really is one."

"There really is," Neil said. "In fact, Graham and I were in it a lot longer than we wanted. We were trapped."

Crescent looked at him in alarm. "Trapped! What happened?"

"Don't worry, it turned out all right," Neil said, as they reached the shore. "I'll tell you about it later."

Mrs. Ruff stared, aghast, when she saw the crowd approaching the back door of the kitchen. "If those people think they can tramp all over my castle," she said to Leonard, "they've got another think coming." As she strode to the door, Leonard slipped quickly away to avoid the confrontation.

"Hi, Mrs. Ruff," Daniel said, before she had a chance to speak. "This is my grandmother and my grandfather."

"So nice to meet you, Mrs. Ruff," Mrs. Lonsberg said. "I do hope the boys haven't been a nuisance."

Mr. Lonsberg extended his hand. "Delighted to be here, Mrs. Ruff. I've heard so much about your castle."

Mrs. Ruff put out her hand, somewhat hesitantly, and Mr. Lonsberg seized it enthusiastically. "We live in New York, you see, Mrs. Ruff, and I knew the original owner of the castle, when he was building it way back when, before the poor man fell on hard times. My, but he couldn't talk about anything else but his castle." He stepped back to gaze up at the towering structure. "Now I can understand why. It's so impressive. May we come in a minute?"

Mrs. Ruff's demeanor had undergone a distinct change. "Why, *uh*, yes," she said. "Come in. Come in." She held the door open.

"This is our friend, Crescent Savage," Mr. Lonsberg said, as they filed in, "and our invaluable fishing guide, Charlie Milton."

"I met Crescent before," Mrs. Ruff said. "And Charlie and I have known each other for a dog's age, haven't we, Charlie?"

"'Deed we have, Ruby," Charlie said. "But what's this I hear about finding the secret passage to the river? You're a sly one, Ruby, you've been holding out on us. I hope you're going to let us see it."

"Why, of course, Charlie," Mrs. Ruff said. "But you'll get a shock when you do. Have the boys told you?"

"We haven't had a chance yet; they just arrived," Daniel said.

"You'd better sit down then," Mrs. Ruff said, pulling up some extra chairs to the big kitchen table. "I'll get some tea while they tell you what they found."

Graham did most of the talking. He told about Daniel pulling the horse's tail, the trapdoor opening to reveal the skeleton, who they thought it was, the POWs tying up Daniel, and Neil swimming out of the tunnel. He didn't, however, mention the shoes Neil had seen in the water – that was something he was going to demand that Sergeant Simpson investigate. Until he found out more, though, he didn't want to speculate about whose shoes they might be.

Then, while they waited for the sergeant to return, Mr. Lonsberg persuaded Mrs. Ruff to describe what it was like in the castle in the old days.

TWENTY-SEVEN

When Sergeant Simpson arrived back at the castle with the coroner, he was surprised to hear chatter coming from the kitchen, as if there was a social gathering in progress. He found a crowd of people sitting around the kitchen table drinking tea, while Mr. Lonsberg and Mrs. Ruff swapped stories about the Roaring Twenties.

"The things I could tell you about some of them high-society folks that came to the castle back then," Mrs. Ruff was saying, when she looked up and saw the policeman standing in the doorway. "*Ah*, there you are, Sergeant. I kept the boys here, like you said. But these folks came looking for them, so I thought they should stay too."

Mr. Lonsberg got up and introduced himself, his wife, Crescent, and Charlie. The sergeant nodded at each of them. Charlie said, "Hey, Simmie, how's it going?"

"Fine, thank you, Charlie," replied the sergeant, trying to maintain the dignity he felt his position called for.

"I've known Simmie since Grade One," Charlie told them. "Never thought he'd turn out to be a police-man. He was a heller back then. Why, I remember the time –"

"The coroner's waiting in the other room," the sergeant said quickly. "He's here to examine the skeleton. You'd better come with me, Ruby. He may have some questions for you."

When he reached the circus room, the sergeant was nonplussed to discover not only Ruby Ruff, but all the others as well, crowding in behind her. Before he could react, Daniel was explaining to the coroner how he'd accidentally pulled the horse's tail and discovered the trapdoor, and Charlie was saying he'd been hearing rumors of a secret passage for years, but it took these boys to find it. There wasn't much the sergeant could do but fade into the background while the coroner took over.

"Right then, open her up," Dr. Patterson said, as if he were talking about a patient on the operating table.

Daniel yanked the tail, and those who hadn't seen it before watched in fascination turning to horror as the trapdoor swung slowly upright, revealing the skeleton. The coroner bent to examine it.

Graham spoke up. "The trapdoor is on a timer, Doctor. The power should be turned off, or it will close again in a few minutes."

"See to that, Sergeant, will you?" Dr. Patterson said. "And bring me a flashlight."

Looking somewhat bewildered, Sergeant Simpson said in a quiet voice, "Do you have a flashlight, Ruby? And, *uh*, where exactly is the main power switch?"

"No need to shut off all the power, Sergeant," Neil said. "Just take out the fuse for circuit thirty-three. Would you like me to show you where it is?"

"No!" the sergeant snapped. "That won't be necessary." He left with Mrs. Ruff, and, a short time later, the lights in the room went out. He returned with a flashlight, which he handed to the coroner. It was the one, Neil saw, that he and Graham had used in the tunnel until the batteries went dead, but he decided he'd better not mention that.

The coroner switched the flashlight on. Nothing happened. He sighed impatiently. "Dead batteries! A fine situation, Sergeant. Don't the police have flashlights that work, for heaven's sake?"

The sergeant reddened. "I, *uh*, didn't think that –"

"It's okay, Simmie, I always carry one with me," Charlie said. He produced a flashlight from one of his voluminous pockets, untangled an assortment of fishhooks and line, and handed it to the coroner.

"It's obviously a child," the coroner said, when he finished his examination. "Hard to tell the exact age or how long it's been there. A decade perhaps – I need to study it more thoroughly in the laboratory. I'll send some men to pack it up properly. There'll have to be an inquest." He shone the light down the stairs. "Anything else I should see down there while I'm here, Sergeant?"

The sergeant shook his head. "It's just a tunnel leading to the river."

"You've been all through it?"

"*Uh* . . . no, but –"

"How do you know then? Maybe there's some evidence down there that would tell us what happened. Or even another skeleton."

"But these two boys said they'd been as far as they could go," the sergeant protested. "The river end of the tunnel is flooded, you see, Doctor, and –"

"Go and look for yourself, Sergeant," the doctor said. "And be quick about it. I haven't got all day." He fished a watch from his vest pocket and frowned at it.

"I'll come with you, Simmie," Charlie said. "You'll need my flashlight."

Grudgingly, the sergeant agreed, and the two of them disappeared down the stairs.

While they were gone, the coroner learned what he could about the history of the castle and the previous owners from Mrs. Ruff and Mr. Lonsberg, paying particular attention to the story of the missing boy. He kept pulling out his pocket watch and checking the time. "Taking them long enough," he grumbled. "I'm a busy man."

Finally the sergeant returned with Charlie.

"Well, find anything?" the coroner demanded impatiently, when the sergeant's head popped up above the trapdoor.

"Just these shoes," Sergeant Simpson said, and he produced a pair of low-heeled, leather woman's shoes. "I found them in the water at the far end of the tunnel."

"Why, those are Miss Stone's!" Mrs. Ruff said.

TWENTY-EIGHT

They all stared at the shoes, as if expecting them to speak up and explain themselves.

"How would Miss Stone's shoes get there?" Mrs. Ruff said. "She's never been in the tunnel – she didn't even know there was a tunnel, none of us did. . . . Heavens, you don't suppose . . . ?"

"The current would have carried them in, Ruby," Charlie said. "It sweeps right by the cave. There's all kinds of stuff washed in down there – candy wrappers, cigarette packages, you name it."

Graham felt sick. He turned to Sergeant Simpson. "Now will you believe me and bring in a police diver?"

"*Hmm*," the sergeant said. He was running out of excuses. "Still, a pair of shoes doesn't prove anything. They might have been accidentally kicked off the dock, or lost from a boat."

"But . . . ," Graham turned to appeal to the coroner, "Doctor, don't you think there should be an investigation?"

"Not my business," the coroner said. "Up to the police. I only deal in dead bodies." He looked at his watch again and briskly packed his bag.

"Your aunt is an excellent swimmer," Mrs. Ruff reminded Graham. "She must have dropped her shoes in the water by accident, that's all. She's probably enjoying the sun somewhere down south by now."

Graham didn't look convinced. Neil could tell by his grim expression that they had more detective work on Deadman's Island ahead of them.

"You can turn the power back on so the trapdoor closes, Sergeant," the coroner said. "And keep it closed until my men get here. I don't want anyone touching that skeleton."

Neil watched the trapdoor descend over the skeleton again. The eye sockets seemed to be staring up at him in mute appeal.

As the coroner headed for the door, Neil followed him out. "Sir," he said, when they were out of earshot of the others, "could I ask you something?"

The doctor stopped. "Yes, what is it?" Again he pulled out his pocket watch. "Make it snappy."

"The thing is, sir, I promised the boy he would be returned to his family."

The doctor frowned. "What boy?"

"The boy in there . . . you know, on the stairs."

"You mean the skeleton?"

Neil nodded.

"Let me get this straight," the doctor said brusquely. "You promised a skeleton, which has been lying there for a decade or so, that it would be returned to its family – whoever they are?"

"It was its . . . *uh*, its spirit, I promised. You see, sir, I have a feeling it's still here – the spirit, I mean. Probably because the boy thought he'd been abandoned and nobody wanted him, so when he died, his spirit didn't go wherever it is spirits go. It stayed here, sort of a lost soul. . . . So I was hoping, after you were through examining his skeleton, you could send it home for a proper burial."

"I see." The coroner's expression softened. "Well, the police will have to locate the family in any case, so . . . I'll tell you what . . . Neil, is it? I'll see that the skeleton is packed up and sent to them for burial, if the family is willing. I promise you that."

"Thank you," Neil said.

"No, thank *you*," the coroner replied. He tucked his

watch back in his vest pocket and walked slowly away, turning back once to look at the boy standing in the hallway.

"I'll need a statement from each of you," Sergeant Simpson said officiously, producing his battered note-book. "And your addresses and phone numbers. You may be called upon as witnesses if there's an inquest." No one really expected that to happen, but the ser-geant wasn't taking any chances – he was already in the coroner's bad books.

"I'll talk to you – one at a time – in the kitchen, starting with Mrs. Ruff," he said. "The rest of you, wait here until I send for you."

As they left the room, Neil heard Sergeant Simpson tell Mrs. Ruff that he'd phoned two of the owners to tell them about the skeleton. Snyder and Grimsby both denied any knowledge of the underground passage or the skeleton. However, they'd agreed to meet the ser-geant there the following day for a routine interview.

While they waited their turn with the sergeant, Graham stood apart from the others, looking forlorn. Neil went over to him. "Are you all right, Graham?"

"It's those shoes," Graham said. "Now I'm sure something's happened to Aunt Etta, and it's all my fault. If I'd come sooner, I could have warned her." He stared out the window. "She used to drop in at our house on her way to meetings. She was constantly hurrying somewhere – the Historical Society, council meetings – but she always took the time to ask me about school before rushing out again."

"Don't blame yourself," Neil said. "You came as soon as you could. Besides, we don't know anything for sure."

Graham shook his head. "I knew those guys were up to something, and I didn't warn her."

No point in arguing with him, Neil thought. Graham would have to work this out himself. "What's done is done," he said. "Now we have to find out if anything *did* happen to her on the island, and if so, what. If we don't do it, no one will."

Graham turned away from the window. "You're right. That sergeant certainly isn't going to, so it's up to us. And if Aunt Etta was attacked on the island, there must be clues somewhere. Which means we've got to keep looking – despite having to cope with Mrs. Ruff."

"Maybe we can get her on our side."

"That'll take some doing, the way she feels about me."

True enough, Neil thought. And they'd have to avoid being seen by Grimsby or Snyder when they arrived.

Mrs. Ruff came back from the kitchen and announced it was Charlie's turn with the sergeant. Neil noticed that she then went off in a corner with Crescent and the two of them had their heads together, talking.

Neil, Graham, and Daniel were the last to be interviewed. Sergeant Simpson called them in together.

"I've already heard all I want to from you three," he said. "Mr. and Mrs. Lonsberg, however, seem convinced you're not troublemakers – though where they get that idea, I don't know – so I'm not going to press the trespassing charges. You're free to go," he added reluctantly.

After the sergeant left, Mrs. Ruff heaved a great sigh. "What a shock finding that skeleton!" she said, to no one in particular. "And to think of all the times I've mopped that floor and the poor boy's skeleton right there underneath it. And then finding Miss Stone's shoes in the tunnel . . . I just wish she'd left a forwarding address, so I could make sure she's all right."

Amen to that, Neil thought.

TWENTY-NINE

They said good-bye to Mrs. Ruff and made their way to the cove, where the launch was anchored. Charlie squinted at the sun, which was halfway down the western sky. "I guess it's too late to do much fishing today," he said.

"I don't feel like it anyway, after seeing that unfortunate child's skeleton," Mrs. Lonsberg said. "You might as well take us back to the cottage, Charlie. Crescent and the boys can come with us, too."

"Actually," Graham said, "I'd like to stay another night at the campsite on Lovesick Island."

Mrs. Lonsberg looked at him in surprise. "But won't your parents be expecting you home?"

"It's okay. I told them we might stay longer if the weather was good," Graham said.

"And I'll stay with him," said Neil.

Then Daniel spoke up. "I'd like to stay too. I'm getting to like camping, believe it or not."

Good for Daniel, Neil thought. He knows we're going to keep investigating, and he wants to be part of it. Besides, if he's here, he's not with Crescent.

"But, Daniel," his grandfather said, "there's been a change in our plans. We have to leave next week to get back to New York."

"We do?" Daniel said, surprised. "I thought we were staying all summer."

"I got a call from Washington yesterday," Mr. Lonsberg said. "The government wants some of us retired folks to come back to help with the war effort. 'Dollar-a-year men,' they're calling us. I'll be looking for missing freight cars carrying everything from ammunition to airplane engines."

"Hey, that's neat, Gramps," Daniel said.

"Your grandfather's going to be doing an important job," Mrs. Lonsberg said. "Do you know that freight cars get lost regularly, and nobody knows where they are?"

"Like lost children, you mean?"

"Sort of," his grandfather said. "Sometimes cars get shunted onto sidings by mistake and left there. I'll be like a train spotter, out looking for them. Anyway, I'm proud to help our country – somehow it didn't seem right to be up here fishing all summer when my country's been attacked. But it means we have only a few more days of fishing. You don't want to miss your last chance to catch a big bass, do you?"

"*Uh*, thanks, Gramps," Daniel said, "but I kind of like camping on Lovesick. Maybe I'll leave the fishing to you and Gran."

"Well, all right," his grandfather said. "But don't go bothering that nice Mrs. Ruff."

"Will you be coming with us?" Mrs. Lonsberg asked Crescent.

"Yes, please," Crescent said. "I'll have to come back again tomorrow, though. I have a job now – helping Mrs. Ruff in the castle."

This declaration surprised everyone.

"A job here!" Neil exclaimed.

"A job helping Mrs. Ruff!" Graham exclaimed.

"A job in the castle!" Daniel exclaimed.

"Really, dear," Mrs. Lonsberg said, "this is very sudden. But, of course, we'll be happy to bring you back again tomorrow."

What's this job all about? Neil wondered, as he

began ferrying the Lonsbergs, Charlie, and Crescent to the launch in the little dinghy. He managed to arrange it so that Crescent was the last to go. "So, what's up?" he asked, as soon as she stepped into the dinghy.

"I had a chance to talk to Mrs. Ruff while we were waiting for the sergeant to finish the interviews," Crescent said. "He'd told her that Grimsby and Snyder agreed to come tomorrow, and she was saying how she hated it when they were there – all the extra work and the service they demanded, especially Mrs. Snyder, who's coming too. So I said I was looking for a summer job and asked if she'd be interested in a helper while they were here. She liked that idea. 'If they want service, let them pay for it,' she said."

Neil stopped rowing and let the dinghy drift. "I didn't know you were even looking for a job."

Crescent smiled. "I wasn't. But I know that you and Graham are really worried about his aunt, and I am too – something's terribly wrong here. You can't risk being seen on the island when Grimsby and Snyder are there – they know you, but they don't know me. So I can be there, helping Mrs. Ruff and watching what they're up to. A spy on the inside, you might say."

"Gosh, you're way ahead of me," Neil said. He gazed at her with a mixture of admiration and concern. "But those guys are dangerous. I don't like it – it's risky."

Crescent touched his hand where it rested on the oar. "Don't worry, sweetie. I'll be in a perfect position to do a little eavesdropping without arousing their suspicion. I want to learn the truth as much as you and Graham."

Then they were at the launch, and Crescent was climbing aboard. Charlie hauled up the anchor and cranked the engine. Neil waved as the launch sped away.

"She called me sweetie," he kept saying, as he rowed back to shore. And he'd been worried about Daniel moving in on him. . . .

There was, however, one cloud on his horizon. Crescent was embarking on a tricky mission, and Neil wasn't sure she realized the extent of the danger. Grimsby worried him the most – he was the ruthless one, the one who'd engineered both of Graham's near "accidents." And the frustrating part was, he'd be stuck at the campsite on Lovesick, unable to help her as long as Grimsby and Snyder were there.

He watched the launch disappear around the point and gave Crescent one last wave. Then Graham and Daniel got in the dinghy with him, and he rowed over to the campsite on Lovesick to spend the night.

THIRTY

Crescent smoothed the quilted bedspread and stood back to admire the four-poster bed she had just finished making. She'd never seen anything like it before – the intricately carved and polished bedposts, the embroidered velvet side curtains, the array of plump pillows.

It was apparent that the elaborate bed, the matching night tables and dressers, the antique pigeonhole desk, and the other furnishings in the Snyders' bedroom were the pick of the castle. Crescent wasn't surprised. From what she'd heard from Mrs. Ruff, Barbara

Snyder made it known that only the best was good enough for her.

That morning, Mrs. Ruff had informed Crescent that the Snyders were taking the morning sun down on the dock and that this was a good time for her to make up their bedroom. It suited Crescent fine – it was just the sort of opportunity she'd been hoping for.

After making the bed, Crescent went straight to the desk – feeling guilty for snooping, but telling herself that this was a necessary part of discovering the truth. Her search of the pigeonholes revealed only shopping lists, invitations, and a few personal letters. The drawers below were jammed with original drawings of the castle, so old they were turning yellow. Nothing of interest there.

Turning to one of the dressers, she was intent on searching through the drawers when she heard voices in the hall. Crescent froze.

The door burst open and a woman in purple shorts and a halter top came in and flung herself into a chair. Her blonde hair and long tanned legs gave an initial impression of youthful glamour, despite the lines around her mouth and eyes.

"It's too hot down there in the sun," she complained to her husband, who followed her in.

Mr. Snyder was a handsome man, with silver gray hair and a golfer's tan. In his bathing suit, however, he looked like he'd been assembled out of mismatched parts – his face and forearms nicely tanned, his chest and stomach sickly white, his legs half and half.

"I do wish you'd tell that lazy clod, Leonard, to put out the sun umbrellas every morning," Mrs. Snyder continued. For the first time she noticed Crescent, who'd quietly shut the dresser drawer and picked up her duster.

Crescent had seen the Snyders from a distance at the Kingsport Yacht Club, but they showed no sign of recognizing her.

"Leave that and bring us a pitcher of ice water," Mrs. Snyder ordered. "And shut the door behind you."

"Yes, ma'am," Crescent said. She was going to have to swallow her pride if she was to play this part well.

"Country girl," she heard Mrs. Snyder say contemptuously, as she closed the door. "She doesn't know enough to leave without being told."

She's probably put out because I didn't curtsy, like some lady-in-waiting, Crescent thought. She purposely lingered in the hall outside the bedroom door. There was no trouble hearing Mrs. Snyder's voice, even through the solid oak.

"I hope you're not going to get cold feet at the last minute again, Carson," Crescent heard her say.

She was unable to catch Mr. Snyder's murmured reply.

"Of course it's necessary," Mrs. Snyder said. "Considering everything you did for the major, he should have left you all of the castle, not a mere one-third. So let's get on with it."

More indistinguishable murmurs from Carson Snyder followed, then the strident voice of Mrs. Snyder again. "No! No more putting it off, Carson. If it's to be done, it must be done quickly."

Crescent heard footsteps coming up the main staircase. She wanted to stay by the door, but now the footsteps were in the hall. She moved briskly away just as a man rounded the corner. Short and stocky, he wore an ugly green sports coat and a gray fedora – a strange outfit for a summer place, Crescent thought. She began dusting the pictures in the hall, and he passed without seeming to notice her, as if she were part of the furniture. She assumed he was the infamous Mr. Grimsby, the man Neil had told her about.

Looking back, she saw him pause by the Snyders' door and raise his hand to knock. He appeared to change his mind and, instead, stood listening for a moment. Then, with a smirk, he continued along the hall to his own room.

"How long will the Snyders and Mr. Grimsby be here?" Crescent asked. She was peeling potatoes in the kitchen, while Mrs. Ruff mixed the ingredients for a cake.

"*Ha*, I wish I knew," Mrs. Ruff grumbled, beating more vigorously, as if it were them in the bowl. "Sergeant Simpson said he wanted to question them today about the tunnel and the skeleton – not that there's anything they can tell him, if you ask me. But, this morning, the sergeant sent a message that he would be tied up all day with the search for the escaped POWs. They still haven't found them."

"At least they found my boat," Crescent said.

With *Discovery* back and undamaged, Crescent had gotten up at first light and sailed to Deadman's Island to start her new job. Rather than making the long sail back and forth every day, she'd asked Mrs. Ruff if she could stay and sleep on her boat.

"Of course, dear," Mrs. Ruff said. "Better than being in the castle at night, at the beck and call of Mrs. High-and-Mighty. Put your boat in the boathouse, where you'll be safer." She grunted with the effort of stirring the stiffening batter. "With Miss Stone not here, I suppose either the Snyders or that Grimsby will be using the castle off and on all summer."

"Or both together?" Crescent said.

"Maybe. Considering the way they used to quarrel, I must say I'm surprised at how well they seem to be getting along this time. 'They fought like cats and dogs when they were here before,' I said to Leonard. 'Not now, though.'"

Crescent dropped a peeled potato into a pot of water and took another out of the basket. She thought back to the Snyders' conversation she'd heard earlier and Grimsby listening at their door. Something was going on between them. Mrs. Ruff thought Grimsby and the Snyders were getting along, but it could all be pretense. Crescent had a feeling they were circling each other warily, neither trusting the other.

She wished she could talk to Neil and Graham about it, but they didn't dare show their faces as long as Grimsby and Snyder were there – they would be sure to be recognized. She was on her own, unless she could find an opportunity to slip away and make the short sail over to their campsite on Lovesick Island.

As the day wore on, however, Mrs. Ruff kept her too busy. And just as she was finishing all the chores she'd been given, Mrs. Ruff sent her into the dining room to polish the silverware.

"Mrs. High-and-Mighty wants to use the sterling silver for dinner," Mrs. Ruff said. "Silver plate isn't good enough for her. Next thing, she'll be wanting to use the Crown Derby dishes and the good crystal glasses for her breakfast."

Crescent sighed and set to work with the silver polish.

Later, she had an early supper at the kitchen table with Mrs. Ruff and Leonard. The Snyders and Grimsby were having drinks on the terrace, after which Mrs. Ruff would serve them dinner and leave. "You can go up and turn down their beds now, and then you're through for the day," she told Crescent.

In the Snyders' room, Crescent turned down the bed and plumped up the pillows. Then she did Grimsby's room. Through the window, she heard laughter and the clink of glasses on the terrace below. Now was the time to search his room for clues.

She went through the desk, but found nothing useful. The dresser drawers were stuffed with clothes – Hawaiian shirts in blaring colors, loud ties, and diamond socks. It was in his underwear drawer that she found the folded piece of paper, carefully tucked into a red-and-white undershirt.

She unfolded it. *Meet me in the tower tonight at twelve*, it said.

Now *that* is interesting, she thought. Who is meeting who in the tower? And why?

She put the paper back, straightened up the drawer, and then headed for the boathouse. There was still an hour or two of daylight. Just time for a quick trip to Lovesick Island to let Neil and Graham know this latest development. Then she would scout out the tower and find a hiding place before midnight. Something was about to happen, and Crescent was determined to find out what.

THIRTY-ONE

"I just hope she doesn't take any chances," Neil said. He'd been fidgeting all day, ever since the Lonsbergs came by in Charlie's boat, en route to another day's fishing. They had dropped off groceries for the boys and brought the news that *Discovery* had been found and Crescent had sailed it to Deadman's Island that morning to start her new job.

Now it was evening, and they were sitting around the campfire – Neil, Graham, and Daniel – roasting the marshmallows they'd found among the groceries, using sharpened sticks.

"Don't worry about Crescent," Daniel said, blowing on his marshmallow, which had caught fire and was rapidly turning black. "She's one smart cookie."

"I know she is," Neil said, annoyed. Did Daniel think he could tell him anything about Crescent? He wanted to tell him off, too, for referring to Crescent as a cookie, but what was the use – that was the way the guy talked. "But you don't know Grimsby. He's dangerous."

"I wonder," Graham put in, "if Grimsby's really the one to worry about."

Neil looked up sharply. "What do you mean? It was Grimsby who tried to run you down in the first place. And when that didn't work, he tried to bean you from the third floor with a flowerpot. If anybody did your aunt in, it was most likely him."

"Agreed, but was it Grimsby who masterminded the whole thing?"

"I doubt it was Snyder," Neil said. "He seems to be the kind who just goes along with somebody else's plan."

"Exactly. So that leaves one other."

"Like I said – Grimsby."

Graham shook his head. "Who has the motivation? That's the key."

"From what you told me," Daniel said, "neither of those two guys dig having to share the castle with your aunt. That's motivation to get rid of her right there."

"*Ah*, yes," Graham agreed, "but who, as you put it, 'digs' sharing the castle the least?" When all he got was blank looks, he answered his own question. "Mrs. Ruff said something interesting the first day we came here. She was telling Crescent about Grimsby and Snyder and what a hard time they give her. 'But the worst of the lot is Mrs. Snyder,' Mrs. Ruff said, and I particularly remember her next remark: 'Thinks she should have the castle all to herself, and wants her husband to get it for her.'"

"Mrs. Snyder!" Neil said. "You think *she's* behind all this?"

Graham nodded. "Lady Macbeth herself. Remember the play, Neil?"

"Yes, but not as well as you," Neil said. "You were in it." Graham had had a walk-on part as one of the castle attendants in the school production.

"You had a part in *Macbeth*?" Daniel said. "Groovy."

Graham shrugged. "A very small part. I just stood around as an attendant. They didn't give me any lines to speak, much to my chagrin. Not even, 'A messenger has arrived, sire.' So I memorized every part in the play, in case someone got sick and they needed a replacement at the last minute. Alas, no such luck."

"You memorized the whole play!" Daniel said. "You are one cool cat."

"So I know the story from front to back," Graham went on, "and it strikes me that it is pertinent to the present situation on Deadman's Island. In the play, we have his ambitious wife urging Macbeth on to murder Duncan so that he will become king – and she queen, of course – but she fears he is too weak-willed to do the job. . . ."

Here Graham jumped up, struck a pose, and quoted Lady Macbeth, "'Yet do I fear thy nature; It is too full of the milk of human kindness.'" He paused theatrically. "See the resemblance? On Deadman's Island, what do we have? Why, Mrs. Snyder, who also wants to be 'queen of the castle,' as Mrs. Ruff so aptly put it, but has a husband who's weak-willed. She's a Lady Macbeth in the making."

"So you think Lady . . . *uh*, Mrs. Snyder might have done in your aunt?" Daniel said.

Graham shook his head. "Read the play. Macbeth gets cold feet about killing the king, but Lady Macbeth urges him on." Again Graham struck a pose and quoted her lines, "'But screw your courage to the sticking-place, and we'll not fail.'"

"Hey, you're good, man," said Daniel. "How come you didn't get a bigger part?"

"The director didn't seem to like me," Graham said. "I can't understand why not – I was constantly offering him advice. Anyway, getting back to the story,

Macbeth finally gives in to his wife's urgings and kills the king. My point being, it's quite possible Mrs. Snyder was the one who talked one of the other two into doing in poor Aunt Etta."

"That could be," Neil said. "It's all speculation, though. We need evidence." He sighed in frustration. "But we can't even go there until they leave."

"*Ah*, but we have our spy," Graham said. "Maybe she'll uncover something."

"Crescent is not our spy," Neil said heatedly. "It was her idea to go there, but I don't like it at all. She'll be in awful danger if they catch her snooping. Look at how they went after you when you found their message in the library book."

But Graham didn't seem to be listening. He was gazing across the water, in the direction of the castle. "Perhaps she's found out something already," he said. "For, if I'm not mistaken, here she comes now."

All three rushed down to shore to greet the approaching sailboat.

THIRTY-TWO

As Crescent nosed *Discovery* up to the public dock on Lovesick, she found three anxious faces peering down at her. "Hi, guys," she said.

She was immediately bombarded with questions.

"Are you all right?" from Neil.

"Found out anything yet?" from Graham.

"Want a roasted marshmallow?" from Daniel.

She climbed out onto the dock. "*Whoa*, give me time to catch my breath. I've had a busy day."

"Yeah, give her a break, you guys," Neil said. "Come and sit by the campfire."

When they had settled by the fire, Daniel toasted a marshmallow for her.

"I can't stay long," Crescent said. "Something's going to happen tonight, and I want to be there." She told them about finding the message in Grimsby's dresser drawer and what she'd overheard earlier outside the Snyders' bedroom.

"You found out all that in one day!" Graham said.

"Yes, but I'm not sure what it all means," Crescent said. "Mrs. Snyder's up to something, but what? And what's this midnight meeting all about?"

"Sounds like she's conned Grimsby into meeting her in the tower," Daniel said, "so hubby can sneak up and stab him, just like that dude Macbeth did."

Graham scotched that idea. "Never. The Snyders are smart enough to know they wouldn't get away with that. It would be too obvious who did it."

"I still think Grimsby's the one to watch," Neil said. "Maybe Grimsby's meeting Snyder in the tower and plans to do him in so *he'll* have the castle all to himself."

"But the note about meeting in the tower was found in Grimsby's room," Graham pointed out. "So I assume it was given to him by one of the Snyders – most likely Mrs. Snyder."

"Man, I'm getting confused," Daniel said. "Who's after who? Reminds me of Abbott and Costello's baseball routine – 'Who's on First?'"

"And just to complicate it more," Graham said, "we're assuming someone's planning murder, but this midnight tryst could be simply a flirtation between Grimsby and Mrs. Snyder."

"Not a chance, Graham," Crescent said. "I saw Grimsby today for the first time, and he definitely wouldn't appeal to someone like her. No, if she's the one who arranged the midnight tryst with Grimsby, then she has something in mind other than romance."

"I bow to your feminine intuition," Graham said. "At any rate, I guess you'll discover what it's all about soon enough."

"I hope so," Crescent said. "The trouble is, whatever happens tonight, we're still not any closer to finding out about your aunt. That's what I was really hoping to learn."

"Maybe you will yet," Graham said. "If you discover who the real villain is tonight, that's the first step."

Dusk was creeping up on them now, turning Deadman's Island into a hulking, formless shape across the stretch of water separating it from Lovesick. Crescent stood up. "I'm off then. I want to scout out the tower before midnight."

"Good luck," Graham said.

Neil took her arm. "I'll walk you to the dock." For a moment, it looked as though Daniel was going to tag along, but Neil's possessive hold on Crescent's arm may have deterred him, for he merely wished her luck and began toasting another marshmallow.

"It's too risky for you, over there all alone. I want to go with you," Neil said.

Crescent shook her head. "No, you stay here. They don't pay any attention to me – I'm just the servant girl. But if they were to see us together . . ." She stepped into her boat. "I'll be careful."

So Neil stayed on the dock, feeling useless, as *Discovery* was swallowed up by the darkness.

When she got back to Deadman's Island, Crescent saw that the lights were still blazing in the castle. She realized that they must still be at dinner. She dropped the sails and paddled into the boathouse, a vast turreted place with enough slips for a dozen boats. Choosing the nearest slip, she tied *Discovery* up snugly for the night. This would be her bedroom as long as she was working here. The slight rocking motion and the slap of water against the side would lull her to sleep. But not tonight. Tonight, she had to stay awake.

On the far side of the boathouse, she could see the dark streamlined shape of a powerboat, the only other craft there. She remembered Mrs. Ruff saying that Grimsby and the Snyders had rented a speedboat from the marina.

Settled down in *Discovery* with a book and a flashlight, Crescent got up frequently to keep an eye on the castle. An hour later, the ground-floor lights began to go out, one by one, and the lights in two of the second-floor bedrooms came on.

Time to go.

THIRTY-THREE

Crescent walked quietly up the path to the castle. The two bedrooms still showed slits of light between drawn drapes.

The full moon lighting her way was so bright that it created shadows. She stopped and looked over at the tower, which dominated the far corner of the castle. It was topped by a tiled conical roof like a dunce's cap, and just below the roof, a balcony overlooked the rocky shore. To get to the tower, Crescent would have to take a circuitous route through the castle.

She followed the path around to the back door and took out the key Mrs. Ruff had given her to access the kitchen. Unlocking the door, she slipped inside.

The safest way to reach the tower, she decided, would be to take the servants' stairs to the empty third floor and cross the floor to the tower.

The bare floorboards of the third floor squeaked beneath her. She stopped, took off her shoes, and continued until she found the door leading to the tower. Almost hidden behind a pile of empty boxes, scrap lumber, and discarded furniture, the door took several hard tugs to open. The unused hinges complained noisily.

Crescent waited until she was sure she hadn't been heard, then slipped through the door and into the tower. She found herself on a landing. Stairs led up from the floor below, and a long narrow window, through which moonlight streamed, illuminated her surroundings. She climbed the stairs that led from the landing to the floor above, stairs so steep that she had to stop and catch her breath at the top. There she found another landing and a door that led out to the balcony. She stepped out cautiously.

The balcony was narrow, with a wrought-iron guardrail that came up to her waist. Her eyes were drawn to the rocks below, where waves rolled in. She shuddered and went quickly back inside.

There was nothing in the way of a hiding place on the top landing. However, attached to the wall opposite the stairs, a metal ladder disappeared into the space under the turret roof – an attic of sorts, perhaps. Crescent considered, then rejected, the idea of hiding up there – she would be trapped, with no way out if she was discovered. She decided it was better to return to the third floor and stay concealed behind the door there. The door had a window, and she could see who went by. Once the two parties, whoever they were, had gone on up to the top floor, she would follow and watch what developed.

Crescent settled down behind the third-floor door to wait, wondering who would be coming up those stairs at midnight. Grimsby, of course, was the one who had received the message. But then who? Mrs. Snyder? If it was her, she would likely arrive late, not wanting to appear too eager. But what they were up to was anyone's guess.

Something rustled behind her, and she swung around. Her flashlight picked out a mouse, peering from the pile of boxes, nose twitching. The mouse stared at her, then scampered away. So long as it wasn't a rat. Rats spooked her.

She returned to her speculations. Neil, bless his innocent heart, couldn't believe that a woman like Mrs. Snyder would be behind these schemes. His theory was that Grimsby was the one to really worry about. The ruthless Grimsby might be plotting something, but in a showdown, Crescent would put her money on Mrs. Snyder.

She tensed as a sound rattled up from below. Footsteps echoed on the stairs, moving up cautiously. She strained to see who was there. A man, she thought, probably Grimsby.

But as the figure crossed the landing and passed in front of the window, the face was outlined momentarily by moonlight. It was Mr. Snyder, much to her surprise. He moved quietly up the final flight of stairs to the top floor.

It was some time before Crescent heard footsteps again. A second shadowy figure appeared from below. This, too, was a man – shorter and stockier than the first. As he passed the window, she saw it was Grimsby. He, too, continued on up.

Now Crescent was thoroughly puzzled. Snyder and Grimsby meeting secretly? Why? What could they be up to that they didn't want Mrs. Snyder to know about? There was only one way to find out.

She drew a deep breath, slipped out onto the landing, and started up the stairs. Suddenly, she heard sounds from below. *Someone else was coming!*

She scrambled back to her hiding place, just as a third shadowy figure appeared. It, too, crossed in front of the window and mounted the final flight of stairs. *Mrs. Snyder*!

Crescent's heart was still beating wildly from her close escape, and she was tempted to stay where she was, behind the third-floor door. She had to steel herself to leave and climb the stairs again, but she did, stopping just short of the top, her head even with the landing.

Through the window in the balcony door, she could see Mrs. Snyder. She was standing at the guardrail and looking out, the moonlight reflecting on her hair. A man's arm circled her waist. Though the man himself wasn't in the frame of the window, Crescent recognized the sleeve of Grimsby's ugly striped sports coat. But where was Mr. Snyder?

Suddenly, Crescent realized that someone was climbing down the metal ladder on the wall across from her. Feet and legs appeared first, then the whole person. Mr. Snyder had been in the attic!

She ducked down the steps as he got off the ladder and crept stealthily across the landing. Reaching the balcony door, he looked through the window at the backs of the two on the balcony. He stood there immobile, his hand on the doorknob.

For what seemed an eternity, no one moved. Not Snyder at the door, not Mrs. Snyder nor Grimsby on the balcony, not Crescent on the steps. The tableau appeared frozen. Then Snyder seemed to stiffen and, throwing open the door, he charged out onto the balcony.

Through the doorway, Crescent saw a turmoil of bodies. She heard a sharp crack, like metal snapping, followed by a long, drawn-out, bone-chilling cry, which faded away and ended abruptly.

The two remaining on the balcony stood silently staring down. Then Snyder, his face contorted, rushed back inside. His wife followed.

"It's done, Carson," she said calmly. "Don't fall apart now."

Crescent took the stairs down two at time, leaping onto the third-floor landing and snatching open the door. But, shaken by that terrible cry of anguish that still rang in her ears, she hadn't reacted fast enough. The Snyders had seen her.

"It's that servant girl – grab her!" Mrs. Snyder cried.

Crescent sped through the door, tripped over the boxes, and sprawled on the floor. Getting herself up, she shoved the boxes, furniture, wood – everything she could lay her hands on – against the door. Then she ran for the servants' stairs.

Behind her, Snyder struggled to open the door. Putting his shoulder to it, he finally burst through, falling into the pile of debris. He lay there cursing, then pushed the debris away, got up, and limped after her. That gave Crescent time to reach the stairs and clamber down. If she got to the boat ahead of him, she could paddle out of reach and raise the sails.

At the bottom of the stairs, she threw open the door and raced across the kitchen.

"Stop right there!" a voice commanded.

Mrs. Snyder was blocking the way to the back door, an evil-looking meat cleaver in her hand. "I'd hate to use this," she said, "but I will if I have to."

THIRTY-FOUR

Neil couldn't sleep. It wasn't the pesky mosquitoes, nor the lumpy ground under him. It was worry – worry about what was happening in the castle and whether Crescent was all right. Where was she now? he wondered. Still in the tower? He didn't have a watch, but knew it must be late as the full moon had traveled halfway across the sky.

Eventually, he decided it was no use lying here wide-awake any longer. He threw back the blanket and made his way to shore, where Daniel's dinghy nestled against the dock, occasionally drifting ahead to nudge its companion, an old abandoned punt part full of water. Neil stared down at the dinghy. Should he or shouldn't he? Was Crescent right? Would it just complicate the situation if he appeared?

Suddenly, the silence of the night was pierced by a faint sound from the direction of Deadman's Island – a muffled shout, or was it a cry of alarm? It ceased abruptly and the silence settled in again, but it was enough to make up Neil's mind.

He untied the dinghy, jumped in, and began rowing frantically, his imagination conjuring up visions of Crescent in trouble. Though there was a slight headwind, he soon reached the other island. Making the dinghy fast to the dock, he stood there, panting from the effort and wondering what to do now.

He looked into the boathouse, where *Discovery* was tied up. Crescent's empty sleeping bag was spread out in the cockpit, a book open on top, but there was no sign of her. He looked up at the tower. Was she still in her hiding place there, waiting? The castle stared back at him, cloaked in darkness.

He took the now-familiar path to the castle. To his right, the tower loomed in darkness. Somehow, he would have to get in there. He crossed in front of the castle and stood looking up at the tower, alert, his ears straining. All he could hear was the rhythmic strumming of crickets.

Now that he was here, Neil began to have second thoughts. Bumbling about in the tower in the dark, he could do more harm than good and might even put Crescent in worse danger. Why had he come, anyway? Perhaps he should wait on the dock for developments. At least he'd be nearby, if she needed him.

But then he caught a glimmer of light reflecting on the trees at the back of the castle. Someone was up. He took the path around to the back. The kitchen light was on. He crept up to a window that was open to the night breeze.

The Snyders were sitting at the kitchen table, and Mrs. Snyder was drumming on the table irritably with her long red nails. Mr. Snyder was slumped over, his head in his hands.

"And we had it all set up so neatly," he groaned. "I mean, Grimsby's supposed suicide note about his money troubles and all. But that servant girl's ruined everything."

"Unless we shut her up," his wife said.

A chill went through Neil.

Mr. Snyder raised his head and stared at his wife. "You don't mean . . . ?"

She met his gaze. "We can't stop now, Carson, not with what we have at stake. We have to change the plan a little, that's all."

"Change the plan? But how?"

"It may even be better this way." Mrs. Snyder was gazing into space, as if already visualizing the success of her new scheme. "Suicide never did suit Grimsby's personality, although I think we would have gotten away with it, from what I hear of that dim Sergeant Simpson. But preying on a servant girl is very much like something Grimsby would do. I can see how it happens now – Grimsby lures the poor girl to the tower under some pretense, grabs her, they struggle, the railing gives way under their weight, they both go over. . . . We find their bodies, one on top of the other, on the rocks below."

"No!" her husband groaned. "I can't do it again. Not another one."

"We've no choice, Carson, we're in too deep now. But you won't have to do it alone. I'll help you."

"I need a drink," her husband said weakly.

She stood up. "Come on then, there's brandy in the library; but only one shot until it's done, then you can have all you want." She nodded towards the pantry. "Check that her knots are holding, then come into the library."

As soon as both Snyders had left, Neil eased the back door open and slipped inside. He found Crescent sitting on the floor of the pantry, her hands tied behind her back and her ankles bound together.

She looked up and her eyes widened in surprise. Neil held his finger to his lips, then quickly found a knife – the same one he'd use to cut Daniel free. Was it only twenty-four hours ago?

He released Crescent and she followed him outside. "Hurry!" he said. "They could be back any minute."

Crescent didn't need any urging. "She had this meat cleaver," she said. "And she looked as if she was ready to use it."

"If we can get *Discovery* underway before they find out you're gone –" Neil began, but there was a sudden shout of alarm from behind them. They ran for the boathouse.

Neil uncleated the lines and jumped aboard, and Crescent began paddling furiously. As *Discovery* glided out of the slip, Neil caught sight of a polished hull glinting in the moonlight on the far side of the boathouse. "Whose boat is that?" he said, in alarm.

"It's theirs," Crescent said, as she hauled up the main. "A speedboat."

Neil's heart did a flip. *A speedboat!* And he thought he'd seen a figure in it. But how could that be? The sounds of pursuit had only now reached the front of the castle. "There they are!" he heard Mrs. Snyder shout.

The sails filled, and *Discovery* slowly picked up speed. *Come on, come on,* Neil urged, but he knew that a sailboat takes time getting up its momentum, unlike a speedboat. He saw Snyder pounding down the path and disappearing into the boathouse. Any second now, he expected to hear the angry roar of the speedboat's motor coming to life.

Carson Snyder was about to leap into the speedboat when he stopped so suddenly that he teetered on the edge of the slip. He stared down in disbelief at the dark shape occupying the driver's seat.

"Come on, get in, Carson," a sepulchral voice said. "Then we can both leave this cursed island forever."

Carson stayed rooted to the spot. "No, no," he quavered. "It can't be!"

"What's this, man?" the voice said. "Don't you want to come with your old friend and partner in crime? I will admit I'm a bit of a mess – my nice jacket's got blood all over it. See?" An arm was lifted toward Snyder, showing the bloodstained sleeve of a sports coat. "Even my face is bloody and my hands. And I'm not as . . . shall we say . . . as substantial as I was before. But that's the way ghosts are – now you see them, now you don't. I'm just getting used to it myself."

Carson backed away, trembling.

The shape in the driver's seat sighed. "Well, if you won't come with me, then I won't go either. And you know what that means – you may own the whole castle, now that you're rid of both of us, but I'll still be here, haunting the halls everywhere you look." The shape laughed – a deep tormenting laugh. "So make up your mind, Carson. . . ."

Carson Snyder turned on his heels and ran from the boathouse, up the path.

At the front door, Mrs. Snyder was waiting to see the speedboat shoot out of the boathouse in pursuit of the disappearing sailboat. Instead, her husband came stumbling back up the path.

"What are you doing here? Get after them, Carson!"

"It's him," Snyder stammered, breathing heavily. "Grimsby!"

"Grimsby! Grimsby! Are you mad?"

"But it's him, I tell you . . . I saw him . . . right there in the boat . . . his jacket all bloody. . . ." Snyder leaned against a column for support.

"Grimsby is dead," his wife said coldly. "Get hold of yourself."

"I know he's dead. . . . It's his ghost. . . . It's going to haunt us. . . ."

Mrs. Snyder delivered a vigorous slap to her husband face. "Snap out of it, Carson. Those two kids in the sailboat are the ones who will haunt us, if they get away. Now listen carefully, I've got everything worked out. You can easily catch up to them in the speedboat. Then you run them down at full speed. . . ."

Snyder looked at her in dismay. "But we can't –"

"Just listen. It happens every summer. The story you tell is simple: you were rushing to shore to report Grimsby's suicide to the police. The sailboat had no lights. You didn't see it until you were on it. Now get going."

"But –"

"Get going."

Snyder returned to the boathouse reluctantly. Approaching the speedboat cautiously, he was relieved to find it empty.

THIRTY-FIVE

In the light breeze, *Discovery* was slow to pull away from Deadman's Island. Neil and Crescent both stared back at the boathouse apprehensively, expecting the speedboat to come flying out at any moment, Snyder hunched over the wheel.

We'll never outrun him, Neil thought. Crescent knew as well as he did that their situation was bleak. Time was what they needed – time to reach Lovesick Island before Snyder caught up to them.

The minutes ticked by, Crescent fiddling with the sails to get more speed, Neil urging *Discovery* on, rocking back and forth, as if that would help. Soon they were halfway.

"Maybe his engine won't start," Neil said hopefully.

"*Something* is holding him up," Crescent said. "Whatever it is, it gives us a chance. Another ten minutes and –"

Vroom, vroom – a powerful engine sprang to life.

"Oh, God, he's coming," Neil said.

Crescent stood up and surveyed the water ahead. "Pull up the centerboard, Neil. Quick!"

He leaped to haul up the board, not stopping to ask why. If Crescent thought it should be done, that was good enough for him.

Still standing, steering with her foot, Crescent pushed the tiller to port. "Found it!" she cried triumphantly.

Found what? Neil wondered. Then he remembered the submerged boulder that Charlie had warned them about.

Behind him, Neil saw the bow wave of the speedboat reflected by the moonlight. It looked like a fluorescent arrow aimed straight at them. On it came, not slowing down in the slightest.

He's going to ram us, Neil thought. There was nothing they could do but brace themselves for the inevitable collision. "Hang on!" he called to Crescent, as the pursuing boat closed in, its prow seeking them out like a predatory shark.

Then, just before it reached them, the speedboat went from full speed ahead to an abrupt, grinding, metal-tearing, shrieking stop, sending Snyder shooting over the windshield. He landed headfirst in the water with a sickening clunk.

Neil stared at the devastation behind them. With the centerboard raised, *Discovery* had cleared the boulder, leading their pursuer into the trap.

Snyder's body was floating facedown in front of the wreckage.

"Jibe, ho!" Crescent called, warning Neil to duck under the swinging boom. *Discovery* jibed through 180 degrees, and they headed back the way they had come.

Crescent maneuvered as close as she could to the wreckage. "I'll get him," Neil said, and he slid over the side and found himself on the boulder in water just above his knees. Grabbing Snyder's heavy body under the armpits, he heaved it into the boat.

They reached Lovesick Island and, with difficulty, lifted Snyder onto the dock. Crescent felt for a pulse. "All we can do is try to revive him here. By the time we sail to the shore and call a doctor, it will be too late."

"It may be too late already," Neil said. "He got an

awful crack on the head and must have swallowed a ton of water."

Crescent began the life-saving technique she'd been taught in swimming classes at the yacht club. Water gushed from Snyder's mouth.

Neil wondered why Graham and Daniel hadn't appeared to help. Maybe they'd slept through the crash and the commotion at the dock. But when he went to the campsite to get them, he found their blankets rumpled from being slept in, but unoccupied.

"Any sign of life?" he said, when he returned. Crescent shook her head. He's a goner, he thought, looking at Snyder's inert body. Still, they had to do all they could to help him, even though he'd deliberately tried to run them down.

Crescent kept working. "Where's Graham? And Daniel?" she said, between breaths.

"I don't know. They were both asleep when I left, but they're not here now. I took Daniel's dinghy over to the castle, so they couldn't have gone anywhere." Then he remembered the old punt, which had been tied up at the dock. It was no longer there. "I can't believe they'd use that leaky old punt!"

But it was only a few minutes later when they heard the squeak of oars in rusty oarlocks, and the old punt came jerkily out of the darkness. Graham was in the stern and Daniel at the oars, having trouble getting the punt to turn toward the dock. "Pull harder on your right oar, Daniel," Neil called. Eventually the punt responded and they reached the dock.

"He's learning," Graham said. "He's a lot better at it than I am." He saw Crescent working on Snyder. "We heard the crash and saw the wreckage; thank God it wasn't you guys. How is he?"

"No sign of life," Crescent said.

Graham and Daniel climbed out of the punt and stood looking down at Snyder. "We should get him to a hospital," Daniel said.

"The wind is dying," Crescent said. "By the time we sail over to shore and find a phone . . ." She got up. "But we'd better go anyway. I don't seem to be doing any good here."

"We should let his wife know first," Graham said.

THIRTY-SIX

They found Mrs. Snyder standing on the dock, peering into the darkness. She watched silently as Neil and Crescent approached in *Discovery*. The wind died completely, and they had to paddle the rest of the way to the dock.

They climbed out. "I'm afraid we have bad news about your husband," Crescent said.

Barbara Snyder looked at the two teens in front of her, her eyes veiled.

How strange, Neil thought, to be standing here with her, when she was making plans just an hour ago to hurl Crescent from the balcony. It felt surreal, as if they were actors in a play discussing the next scene.

"His boat hit a submerged rock and he was thrown out," Crescent said. "I tried to revive him, but . . ."

"He's dead, isn't he?" Mrs. Snyder said in a flat voice.

Crescent hesitated. "I . . . I can't detect any pulse – that's all I know."

"We could take him over to shore now and try to find a doctor," Neil said. "But it will be a long, slow trip with no wind. . . . It might be just as fast to wait till morning, when the Ruffs come with their boat."

"I'd like to see him," Mrs. Snyder said, after a pause.

Neil saw that Daniel's dinghy was still tied up where he'd left it earlier. "Your husband's at Lovesick. We'll leave the sailboat here and row you over."

On the way, they were silent, avoiding each other's eyes. Mrs. Snyder stared at the wreckage of the speedboat as they passed by.

Graham and Daniel were waiting on the dock with the body. Graham was anxious to question Mrs. Snyder about his aunt's disappearance and might have, regardless of the circumstances, had Daniel not convinced him that this wasn't the right moment.

Mrs. Snyder got out and approached the body. They all stood back while she knelt and lifted her husband. For a moment, Neil thought she was going to take him in her arms, but she was only turning him over to check for a heartbeat and examine the gash on his head. When she straightened up, Neil could see that her eyes were moist.

"Take us both back to the island, please," she said. "It's only a few hours till dawn."

They lifted Snyder into the dinghy. There wasn't space to lay him flat on the bottom, so they sat him on the stern seat, his wife beside him to keep him from toppling over. It looked for all the world, Neil thought, as if they were taking a drunk home from a party. He manned the oars and Crescent sat in the bow.

As they approached Deadman's Island, Mrs. Snyder began, for the first time, to speak. "He was a good man at heart," she said. "Weak, though. As long as everything was going well, Carson was fine, but if something went wrong, he fell apart. Do you know, he actually thought he saw Grimsby's ghost sitting behind the wheel of the speedboat tonight?"

So that's why it took him so long to come after us, Neil thought. We were saved by a ghost! He waited to hear more, but Mrs. Snyder turned to the body of her husband.

"I don't suppose I was the best wife for you, Carson," she said, smoothing his hair. "You should have married someone with less ambition, someone who would have been content just being your wife."

"What will you do now?" Crescent said.

Mrs. Snyder considered, then said in the same flat voice, "I shall spend my days in retreat – husbandless and ambitionless."

Neil doubted Mrs. Snyder would ever be ambition-less. Nevertheless, he began to feel sorry for her and had to remind himself what she had done. He thought of Grimsby's broken body, still lying on the rocks. What a shock it will be for the Ruffs – first a skeleton, now two bodies.

When they reached the dock, they lifted Snyder's body out. They expected Mrs. Snyder would want them to carry it to the castle, but she told them to leave it at the dock. "I'd rather not go back to the castle ever again," she said. "That place was our down-fall. I'll just stay here with him and wait for the Ruffs."

As Neil rowed away, the last he saw of Mrs. Snyder, she was sitting on the bench staring out over the water, the body of her husband propped up beside her. "I wonder if she'll be charged over Grimsby's death," he said.

Crescent looked skeptical. "I doubt it. She has her cover story."

"But she can't say it was suicide. She knows that you saw it all."

"Yes, but all I could see was a jumble of bodies on the balcony. I couldn't tell who pushed who, and she knows that. She'll say that her husband was jealous and that he and Grimsby tussled, the railing gave way, and he tumbled over. I couldn't dispute that."

"She's got it all worked out, hasn't she?" Neil said. "I suppose they loosened the railing beforehand too, but I don't expect the cops will catch that – not with Sergeant Simpson doing the investigating. She'll play the bereaved widow, and he'll swallow her story about Grimsby hook, line, and sinker." Neil turned to make sure he was still heading for the Lovesick Island dock. "But it may not be so easy to explain what her husband was doing chasing us with the speedboat."

"I don't know about that," Crescent said. "She can say he must have changed course to avoid hitting us and hit the rock instead. Boating accidents like that happen all the time – especially at night. There's no way for us to prove he was planning to ram us. Anyway, what's the point – he's dead."

Neil made a course correction with an oar. "We're just lucky that Snyder got spooked by a ghost and didn't catch up to us sooner. Otherwise, it might be us laid out on the dock instead of him."

Crescent shuddered. "Don't say that, Neil." She leaned forward and touched his cheek.

"I wonder how come he thought he saw Grimsby's ghost?" he said. "Blood-soaked jacket and all, he told his wife."

"It *is* strange," Crescent said. "Almost as if Grimsby's ghost was looking out for us – if it really was Grimsby's ghost."

Neil stopped rowing. "You don't suppose . . . ?" He gazed at her. "I wonder where Graham and Daniel went in that old punt?"

"A good question," Crescent said. "Where *did* they go, and what were they up to at that hour?"

"I'm going to ask them," Neil said.

But, for the moment, he wanted to forget the events of the night. The water was flat calm, like a dark polished mirror. He let the dinghy drift and patted the seat beside him. "Come and sit here."

She slid into the seat and he folded her in his arms. The dinghy continued to drift, the two figures locked as one, a ribbon of moonlight stretching out before them like a silver path.

THIRTY-SEVEN

It was driving Neil nuts. All he could get out of Graham were meaningless responses, accompanied by an enigmatic grin. Nor was Daniel any more forthcoming.

"C'mon, Graham," Neil pleaded. "Did you or didn't you impersonate Grimsby's ghost last night?"

"But Neil, to impersonate means to imitate a person," Graham said, "and a ghost is not a person – at least not anymore. Therefore it's a contradiction in terms, if you see what I mean. . . ."

"Oh, for Pete's sake. All right then, I'll rephrase my question. Did you find Grimsby's body and borrow his sport's coat? Then did you get in the speedboat and pretend you were Grimsby's ghost in order to scare off Snyder?"

"What! Take a bloody sport's jacket off a dead man and put it on? Yuck! I shudder at the thought. Besides, it's highly illegal to tamper with a dead body before the police arrive. Think what Sergeant Simpson would say if he suspected I'd undressed Grimsby's corpse and borrowed his clothes!"

Neil sighed. They were sitting around the campfire, only smoldering ashes now. Crescent, however, had returned to Deadman's Island. She had grown fond of Mrs. Ruff and knew she would need company after the shock of finding two bodies.

Leonard, accompanied by Mrs. Snyder, took Snyder's body to shore. Grimsby's, however, was left untouched to await the arrival of Sergeant Simpson.

The morning sun and the blue sky proclaimed yet another fine day. Gulls circled raucously around a boiling school of minnows. The world goes on as if nothing happened, Neil thought, no matter what people get up to in the night.

He turned back to Graham. "If you were impersonating Grimsby, you're a hero in my books. By delaying Snyder, you saved Crescent and me – otherwise he would have caught us and run us down."

"What difference does it make who saved you?" Graham said. "All that matters is that you were saved."

"But don't you see? If *you* didn't do it, and *Daniel* didn't do it, it means there really was a ghost!"

Daniel said, "Don't you believe in ghosts? I sure do. My great-grandmother's ghost is still hanging around Gran and Gramps' house on Long Island. She's neat."

"I don't know whether I believe in ghosts or not," Neil said earnestly. "That's what I'm trying to find out. But you guys aren't helping at all."

"Sometimes it's best to retain your illusions," Graham said. "Especially in these times."

And that was all Neil could get out of him. Graham was, understandably, more concerned about his aunt. "With Grimsby and Snyder gone, I wonder if we'll ever find out about Aunt Etta," he said morosely. "I don't imagine Lady Macbeth will tell us anything. If she is involved with Aunt Etta's disappearance – and I'm darn sure she is – she'll never admit it. She'll be more interested in saving her husband's reputation, as well as her own. But I'm still going to try to get Sergeant Simpson to grill her about it."

He stood up and stretched. "I'm going down to the dock to wash up."

Graham was kneeling on the dock, washing his hands and face, when he heard the whine of an outboard. He looked up. A small runabout was going by, headed for Deadman's Island. He did a double take and looked at the woman in the yachting cap running the out-board. *Could it be?* Impossible. *But yes, it was!*

He leapt up. "Aunt Etta!"

Henrietta Stone looked around to see where the voice had come from.

"Over here!" he called, and she, in turn, did a double take when she spotted Graham dancing around the dock and frantically waving his arms. She veered her boat sharply and headed for Lovesick.

"Graham! What a coincidence running into you here," she said, as she pulled into the dock.

Graham was stunned by the sight of her. "Are . . . are you all right, Aunt Etta?" he managed to say.

She scrambled nimbly onto the dock. "Of course I'm all right. Why wouldn't I be?"

He had an urge to throw his arms around her and hug her right then and there, but he couldn't quite do it, as much as he cared for her – neither he nor his aunt were huggers. He was so overcome to see her, however, that tears welled up. He turned away and swiped at his eyes.

"What a lovely surprise," his aunt said. "What are you doing here?"

"Camping, Aunt Etta," Graham said, still some-what stunned.

"That's my castle over there." She pointed. "Hard to believe it belongs to your aunt now, isn't it? I can hardly believe it myself. You may have heard about the horrendous events there last night."

"I'll say I did," Graham began, "in fact, we –"

"I'm just going there now to find out more. Both Grimsby and Snyder dead in terrible accidents. Heavens! I'm not ashamed to admit I didn't like either of them, but I wouldn't have wished their fate on anyone. At any rate, it's safe to return now, callous as that may sound."

"Safe to return?" Graham said. "Then you knew –"

"Of course I knew them. They're the other two owners of the castle – they *were* the other two owners, I should say. Now I'm the only one left."

"What I meant was –"

"Confidentially, Graham," Henrietta looked around to make sure no one was listening, "they were not nice men. I believe they sabotaged my boat. Certainly, someone did. It sank under me in the middle of the channel last Sunday."

"Your boat sank! What did you do?"

"Why, I swam to shore, of course."

"But Aunt Etta, that's a long way! How did you ever –"

"I swim almost that far every day," Henrietta said indignantly, as if her prowess had been doubted. "Quite a current, mind you, and carrying my purse around my neck made it a bit difficult. I wanted to save my good shoes too, but they slowed me down and I had to kick them off – they were practically new. So I had to buy new ones, and I also bought this yachting cap – rather chic, don't you think? I can't wear my favorite straw hat when I'm in the boat – it blows off and I have to chase it."

Two more puzzles solved, Graham thought. "But where did you go when you got ashore?" he managed to slip in. "We were looking –"

"Why, I just drove down the road to the Riverview Inn. Charming old place. I thought of going to the police about the sabotage, but I had no proof – the boat is now on the bottom – so I decided the safest thing was to let Grimsby and Snyder think they'd succeeded in getting rid of me. I knew they wouldn't tell anyone, of course, so I didn't have to be concerned that my friends would be worrying about me. But I vowed I'd never stay in the castle again while they were there. I thought I'd just wait until they'd gone back to town, then I'd rent another boat at Muldoon's, come back to the castle, get my suitcase and clothes, and leave on my trip south, as I planned all along. But when I heard about the deaths here last night, that changed everything."

She shook her head. "Hard to believe, both of them in one night. People in Riverview are saying it's the curse of the castle again. I suppose nobody will ever know what really happened."

"Actually," Graham began. "Neil and Crescent and I –"

"Your friend Neil is here? And Crescent too? Lovely girl. How nice, the three of you together on a camping trip. But what a coincidence! Here you are, camping right across from my castle – I guess I can call it my castle now that I'm the only one left. You must come over and I'll give you a tour. It's an intriguing place. You'll love it. And bring your friends – they'll enjoy seeing it too."

Graham sighed. "I'm sure they will, Aunt Etta."

"Well, I must be on my way," Henrietta said. She leapt back in her boat and cranked the outboard into life. "I'm so glad I ran into you, Graham," she shouted over the roar of the motor.

"I'm glad you did, too," Graham shouted back. "In fact, you'll never know how glad I am."

"Now what do you suppose he meant by that?" Henrietta said to herself, as she opened the throttle wide and shot off. "Lovely boy, young Graham, and very bright. He's certainly different, though. For a moment there, I thought he was going to cry. Perhaps he's homesick. I do hope he comes over to see me."

Graham stared after the speeding runabout until it turned into the boathouse on Deadman's and disappeared. When the sound of the outboard died away, he had to keep telling himself that the brief encounter with his aunt hadn't been a figment of his imagination.

Neil and Daniel came down to the dock. "We heard voices," Neil said, looking around. "Was someone here?"

Graham turned to them. "To quote the messenger in the last act of *Macbeth*, when he saw the trees of Birnam Wood move, 'Gracious my lord, I should report that which I say I saw, but know not how to do it.'"

"*Huh?* You feeling all right, Graham?" Daniel said.

Graham smiled. "I'm great, thanks, and this calls for a celebration. Let's go toast some marshmallows for breakfast and I'll tell you all about it."

The End

AFTERWORD

Though there are several actual castles in the Thousand Islands, the castle in this story is fictional, as is Deadman's Island, on which it is set, and nearby Lovesick Island. There is a Deadman's Bay and a Lovesick Lake in Southern Ontario, and the author has taken the liberty of borrowing their singular names.

Find out what else is In the Cards in:

Love

Fame

Also by Mariah Fredericks

Crunch Time

Head Games

The True Meaning of Cleavage

In the Cards
Life

Mariah Fredericks

ALADDIN MIX

NEW YORK   LONDON   TORONTO   SYDNEY

ALADDIN MIX

Simon & Schuster Children's Publishing Division

1230 Avenue of the Americas, New York, NY 10020

Text copyright © 2008 by Mariah Fredericks

Illustrations copyright © 2008 by Liselotte Watkins

All rights reserved, including the right of reproduction in whole or in part in any form.

ALADDIN PAPERBACKS and related logo and ALADDIN MIX and related logo are

registered trademarks of Simon & Schuster, Inc.

Designed by Ann Zeak

The text of this book was set in ITC Legacy.

Manufactured in the United States of America

First Aladdin MIX edition April 2009

2 4 6 8 10 9 7 5 3 1

The Library of Congress has cataloged the hardcover edition as follows:

Fredericks, Mariah.

Life / Mariah Fredericks. —1st ed.

p. cm.

"A Richard Jackson book."

Summary: Syd, who is much more comfortable with animals than people, asks her friends for a tarot
reading, then fears the dire predictions are coming true as her parents fight, her aging cat suffers, and
her friendships are tested.

ISBN-13: 978-0-689-87658-5 (hc)

ISBN-10: 0-689-87658-0 (hc)

[1. Family problems—Fiction. 2. Friendship—Fiction.

3. Self-esteem—Fiction. 4. Bashfulness—Fiction. 5. Tarot—Fiction.

6. Fortune telling—Fiction. 7. Manhattan (New York, N.Y.)—Fiction.]

I. Title.

PZ7.F872295Lif 2008

[Fic]—dc22

2007034125

ISBN-13: 978-0-689-87659-2 (pbk)

ISBN-10: 0-689-87659-9 (pbk)